Jacet

Jenny 2018

Print Edition
ISBN: 978-0-9981052-6-0
Published by Amie McCracken, 2017

Cover and interior design by Amie McCracken
Cover image from Christopher Meder

To the Sea

edited by Amie McCracken

anthology from the writer's playground
all proceeds donated to the ministry of stories

Table of Contents

To all those who gaze in wonder at the sea and let their imagination float away in search of the tales darting among the waves.

The Claiming

Amie McCracken

We never wanted children. Living in our secluded cabin, backed by dark, mossy woods and facing the turbulent sea, enjoying life, each other, solitude. I had space and time, all I needed to work on my sculpting. Lain had a getaway to escape to every evening when he came home from his life-altering lab. We had discussed not ever having children, many times. It was a decision we had made separately and together, to focus on our pursuits and keep life as it was. But one day he came to me and proposed adopting a changeling. His employer, Emodiant, had put a call out for suitable candidates for a new set of experiments. The first round of changeling children were ready to join the real world, and Emodiant wanted to see how they would fare in stable homes with two norm parents. We fit the bill.

We spent weeks debating. A changeling wouldn't be the same as a normal child. It wouldn't set the demands and requirements that we saw as shackles to our freedom. But it still meant caring for a creature other than ourselves. Plus, what did it mean to raise a changeling? They grew, cognitively and physically, at an increased rate. They were void of feeling, having no hormones, so we wouldn't need to coddle them, but we also *couldn't* coddle them. There was no rule book, no instructions for how to take on this task. And while we felt, being an artist and a scientist, that we had the capacity to learn and adapt and overcome, we were still human.

I sat one evening, mulling this all in my head, while my hands mechanically did the work for me, of molding and manipulating the clay. It wasn't a decision I particularly wanted to make. A child was like the clay in my hands, warm and pliable. A changeling was more like a piece of wood, still receptive but hard and stiff. Or even worse, like a piece of metal, requiring cutting and welding to create something new. Especially since our option was to adopt a child who was five years old in rounds of the Earth, but more like twelve or thirteen, intellectually. I was so lost in my thoughts and the soft feel of the clay on my fingers that I didn't hear the car arrive, or Lain come through the door.

"Joca?" he called.

I jumped.

"In the studio," I said, after a moment to collect myself. Then I wiped my hands on my rag and stood to face him as he walked in.

"Hello," he said and walked right over to kiss me. His finger came to my cheek and gently wiped away a smudge of clay. "What's for dinner?"

"I thought we could make spaghetti from scratch. I bought fresh ingredients."

"That sounds excellent. I'll pour some wine. Shall I turn on music?"

"Maybe not tonight," I said, my head still rumbling with thoughts. "Let's open the doors and listen to the waves. I'll be right behind you."

I put the studio to rights and followed him through the walkway into the main part of the house. It was one large room, with a bedroom and bathroom to one side, my studio and another bedroom to the opposite. He had lit a fire to combat the breeze coming through the doors.

We settled in to making dinner, in silence. It wasn't a time to talk. He needed to recharge, and I wasn't sure what to say anyway. I had still not come to a place I felt I could be comfortable with. I wanted to change the world. I wanted to make a difference. And the work Lain did with Emodiant was headed that direction. So by taking in a changeling, by being part of their experiment, wasn't I making my mark?

We chatted about other things when the food was finished. After the dishes were clean we took our respective books to our respective chairs by the fire and read. When it grew darker outside, Lain took my hand and brought me to the porch. We watched the stars without the moon hindering our view. They sparkled and twinkled as if to garner the most attention possible from us.

"Have you decided?" he asked. "We've run out of time. They have to deliver the child on Monday if we want him." His arms came around me and the warmth was delicious.

"I think I have," I said.

"And?"

"I think we should."

"I agree. It won't be quite like this anymore, but it won't be much different either."

"We'll see," I said.

We had one last weekend to enjoy our privacy from other beings, one last weekend to make love on the bed and then the couch and then make breakfast in the nude. One last weekend for me to sculpt Lain as he lay on the divan in my studio drinking coffee and reading a book.

On Monday morning, his supervisor arrived with the changeling and our world tilted slightly sideways.

Dr. Rooken brought Odi to our house. They stepped out of the car, and Odi immediately looked up at the trees towering over his tiny body. Then he calmly lowered his gaze to mine, said, "Hello," and sauntered up to the porch.

"I hope it's okay that I brought him now," Dr. Rooken said with a smile.

"I didn't realize you would personally deliver him," Lain said. "Would you like a cup of coffee?"

"Sure. Thank you. Come on in Odi," Dr. Rooken said, and we all went inside. I pulled another mug down and made Dr. Rooken a coffee. Odi stood in the kitchen, contemplating. Lain and Dr. Rooken talked, but I didn't hear much. I couldn't take my eyes off the little boy, standing like a young man in a college lecture hall, his head cocked and his face blank.

"Will you be ok?" Lain called through my thoughts. His brows were knitted, a crease formed on his forehead. I wanted to smooth it away.

"Hmm?" I said. "Oh. Of course."

"Thanks again for doing this Joca," Dr. Rooken said. "We'll be interested to see what happens."

"Always the scientist," I said, handing him his coffee. The men continued conversing while I tidied up, and Odi stayed locked in his current position. Then he followed as the men went out the door. He waited on the porch until the car had disappeared from sight. When he came back in, I was prepared.

"Odi, what would you like to do?"

"Your husband didn't want to leave you here."

"Um."

"He's worried about me. Why is that? He didn't seem to be able to pinpoint why."

I tried to remember what Lain and Dr. Rooken had been talking about. I had only caught snippets, but I was pretty sure it was harmless small talk. Where had Odi gotten this idea? From the one comment? From something else? From body language?

"This is a new environment for you. That might be hard for you. That's all," I said.

"Nothing is hard as long as I can learn." His eyes flitted to the table between our armchairs. "Can we play chess?" he asked.

"Yes." I sighed, relieved to have something to do with my hands and mind. I poured more coffee and brought a water glass over for Odi.

We played three games. All of which I lost. Every time I tried a new tactic, Odi figured it out before I fully executed it. I was a skilled chess player, but this was a challenge. I relished it.

"You are acceptable," Odi said. Then he stood and took our glasses to the sink. He dragged a chair over so he could reach and proceeded to wash the rest of the dishes.

Lain spent the evening with it—him—while I went to my studio to decompress and get what work needed doing, done. We had spent the rest of the day in companionable silence: Odi perusing the books on our shelves and enjoying the view from each window for a half hour at a time, me unable to focus on anything other than observing his behavior. Lain got home and immediately took him outside to find sticks for the fire and 'bond', or so he said. I wasn't sure it was the best idea.

The next morning, I caught Lain ruffling Odi's hair on

his way out the door. Odi's face showed no emotion, but I thought I saw a shadow pass over his eyes.

After Lain was long gone, I heard the door open and shut and looked up from my book to find myself alone. Odi had stayed confined to the house yesterday without prompting, but his adventures with Lain seemed to have made him bold. I went after him. But the driveway was empty.

I ran around the side of the house to the front. Nothing. No child. No animals. Not even any wind.

I sprinted to the woodshed. Again, nothing.

The only two options were the path to the hiking trail, which led to the lighthouse, or the driveway out to the road. I made a snap decision and trekked into the forest.

After a half mile hike, calling Odi's name and listening for any kind of response, I reached the clearing that overlooked the bay and the lighthouse, standing on its peninsula in all its crumbling glory. Odi stood on the beach. A gush of air escaped my lips.

"Odi!"

He turned so slowly, so so slowly, an inquisitive look on his face.

"Why would they leave such an outdated building standing? Why wouldn't they tear it down and use the materials for something new?"

I grabbed his shoulder and knelt down.

"Don't ever do that. Don't ever run away without telling me where you're going. I'm okay with you exploring, but I need to know where you are. At all times."

"Okay."

He waited.

I choked on my saliva and wondered if he would be the death of me. My heart was racing. I put a hand to my chest and settled onto my haunches.

"I will not kill you," Odi said.

A shiver ran up my spine.

"What is the purpose of this building?" He gestured at the lighthouse.

"It was a lighthouse, to guide ships to shore during storms and warn them of a rocky area. That was before ships had adequate navigation and autonomy."

I rubbed my arms. They were covered in goose bumps. The wind finally picked up and lashed our hair about.

"Let's go back to the house. And promise me you won't do that again."

"I don't think I should make a promise. But I won't kill you. And I won't go anywhere without telling you again," Odi said and then walked away from me toward the house. "I am going back to the house," he called over his shoulder.

Lain and I woke early on Saturday morning. We lay in bed, waiting to take on the day, next to each other and not touching. I severely needed time alone, in my studio. The week had been exhausting, and I was doubting our decision. Until Lain spoke...

"He's interesting, isn't he?"

I grunted.

"I find it fascinating to watch him analyzing his surroundings and taking in everything. It's an incredible experience to witness a brain growing."

My husband, the constant scientist.

"But it's more than that, isn't it? He's also beautiful, in a way. He has abilities that I wasn't prepared for. Have you noticed?" He turned to me, a broad grin crossing his face.

"Noticed what?"

"How intuitive he is. It makes me wonder if he is capable of love."

"It—he is not. I can tell you that."

"That's harsh. Do you want me to send him back? That wouldn't be very good for his development."

"Lain!" I sat up. "This is basically a machine we're talking about. This is not a child. It—he is methodical and logical and cold. There is nothing there to love. Please tell me you aren't falling in love?" I took his hand and brought it to my cheek. The sun graced our room and lit it golden orange. I heard movement in the kitchen and shivered.

"I..."

I glared at him.

"Look. I'm not falling in love. I'm just enjoying the experiment. I find it fascinating. Okay?" he said. But his eyes flitted to the ceiling as he said it. His cheeks burnished a deep red before he took his hand back and got out of bed. With his back to me, he said, "Take the day in the studio. I'm going hiking with Odi." And then he was gone.

That night I thought I would fall into my bed and sleep. I had been productive, fulfilling three orders from my gallery and preparing ideas for a new show. The three mugs of cold tea sitting on my workbench were a testament to my dedication, but even feeling accomplished and satisfied, I couldn't enter dreamland. I tossed and turned, finally facing the French doors from our bedroom to the back porch, the sea, and the moon beyond. I tried to count the stars.

The hairs on the back of my neck stood on end. I felt chilled. I stood from the bed, shaking in the cold, and walked up to the doors.

Standing at the edge of the porch, in the dark, was a tiny human shadow, barely distinguishable from the pole supporting the roof. His eyes almost glowed.

I smacked the window.

He turned, ever so slowly, and went back to the open door to the living room. I stayed where I was until I heard the click and footsteps taking him back to his bedroom. Then I went to my own bed and spent the night staring at the ceiling, working to calm my heart rate and my breathing.

On Sunday I woke from a few hours' sleep to a headache and an empty bed. There was laughter—Lain's—and the clatter of dishes. I stood in the doorway to our bedroom for a moment, watching Lain attempting to banter and play with Odi while they prepared a large breakfast. Odi did not react back.

The need for coffee overwhelmed my need to observe, so I went straight for a mug.

"It smells delicious," I said. The table was covered in dishes of fruit and pancakes and different sauces.

"It is sustenance," Odi said and sat. He tucked right in without waiting.

"Odi, you need to wait for everyone to sit down," Lain said.

Odi stopped cutting his pancakes and set his fork down, then stared off into nothing.

We sat and dished up food.

"You can eat," Lain prompted. Odi picked up his fork and continued.

"What would you like to do today, Odi?" I asked.

"I am not at liberty to request. We can do whatever you wish," Odi said. I still couldn't get over the fact that words like that were escaping the mouth of what looked like a five-year-old child. He didn't fidget in his seat; he didn't shove food in his mouth and chew in an ungainly manner. He was a proper adult, albeit in a tiny vessel.

Rain started to splatter the windows.

"Joca, you still need some studio time," Lain said and glanced out the French doors. "Odi and I will find things to do in here after cleaning up."

I didn't finish my breakfast. The studio called. I took my mug and disappeared into my private world.

A few hours later though, the sounds of both laughter and frustration greeted my ears. My attention was diverted, though my fingers kept working the clay. And before I knew it, the clay was dry and the semblance of a figurine in my hands snapped. I let the pieces crumble to the countertop and focused my full attention on the voices.

"That's impossible. How did you beat me that time?" Lain grunted and then laughed. "Well, let's go again." I imagined him ruffling Odi's hair. I crept to the door and cracked it to listen.

"I do not want to play again," Odi said.

"I do. I know I can win. One more?" Lain begged. I had never heard him beg anyone for anything. His attachment to Odi was reaching uncomfortable proportions.

"You think that you can win, and I see the strategy already laid out in your head. You cannot beat me. In fact, you are an inferior form and unfit to be a father."

I gasped.

A door slammed.

I stepped into the living room.

Odi stood alone.

"Odi?" I said and stepped into the room.

"He is insufficient."

"Where has he gone Odi?"

"We are better without him."

"No. Where is he?" I ran to the French doors to search the lawn. Maybe he was just standing by the sea. Maybe he was chopping wood. Maybe what I had heard hadn't really happened. My husband was definitely falling in love with this creature, and it had just broken his heart.

There was no sign of him and the storm was picking up. I pulled on a sweater and raincoat and boots. I looked back at Odi, hesitating about leaving him on his own.

"Where did he go?" I asked again.

"Places meant for thinking. Places meant for dying. Places that used to save people."

I shook my head. Had I walked into a horror movie? What was with the cryptic language? I no longer worried about leaving him alone. I put my hand on the doorknob and stepped into the maelstrom.

The wind whipped my hair into whirlpools. It was so strong it made the rain feel like ice chips, biting my cheeks and hands and any available skin. I made a choice, hoping that Odi's riddle meant what I thought it meant, and headed for the lighthouse. When I reached the clearing, the storm paused. Only long enough for me to see a figure standing at the top of the lighthouse.

"No!" I screamed into the wind that picked up again. The glittering sea before my feet frothed. The lighthouse on the other side of the bay swayed and groaned. And behind me I heard the crunch of stones as someone walked by. I turned to find nothing, but the hairs on my arms stood to attention. When I faced the lighthouse again, two figures stood on the porch with no railing—one the size and shape of my husband; one the size of a tiny child.

I started running. But because I watched the scene before me instead of my footing, I tripped on driftwood just as the child pushed the man. I fell as he fell. I landed as he landed, among the rocks, battered and bloody.

I lifted myself to my feet. Odi stood by my side. I jumped.

He held out a hand. "Let's go home, Mother. There's no reason to be out in this weather."

I took his hand and let him lead me home.

Half Sick of Shadows

Jeannie Wycherley

Wande lay on her belly, her toes anchoring her to the red soil of the riverbank, wiggling her fingers in the slow-moving water. The day had been warm, and the sun was still beating down on her, burning the back of her neck. Mayr had told her she would catch more fish here, in the tributary, where the white willows trailed their fronds out of the direct current of the water as it surged for the sea. So far she had snared two small silver fish. Supper, thus far, had eluded her.

Perhaps if she ventured into the water itself?

This was forbidden by her mother, but she couldn't return home empty-handed. Wande scrambled to her feet and waded into the water, ensuring she kept close to the bank. She parted the wands of the willow trees and moved beneath the thick foliage, into the cool shade, intent on better luck.

The stench of death stilled her.

Wande waited for her senses to grow accustomed to the feeling of assault.

Ensnared among low-hanging branches, dead trees, and the detritus of local beavers, was a boat. A small barge. Recently it had sported silk sails, but now only the tattered remnants, bright colours muted and dank with decay, were draped over the stern of the boat, or snagged in branches overhead.

And there was something else. A woman dressed in once-bright, lacy finery lay sprawled across the deck of the barge, her upper body elevated by cushions, her dark hair trailing across them. Her head was turned to the riverbank as though seeking assistance, or perhaps reassurance, in the final moments of her life.

Wande cast her net aside and waded deeper into the water until she was in touching distance of the prow of the barge. She could make out the neat hand-lettering that spoke the name of the vessel and perhaps its lonely inhabitant.

"Wande?" a young man's voice from the bank interrupted the girl's reverie. Mayr, the farmer's boy. Her intended.

"Here," she called, her voice low and reverential. "Under the willows."

A curse, a splash. Mayr's head appeared under from among the feathery tentacles, his expression one of exasperation. "What are you doing in here?" he asked.

"See what I have found," Wande whispered, even as Mayr gazed upon the barge in wonder. "What does this say?" she asked.

"The Lady of Shalott," he read aloud, then whistled. His eyes scrutinized the barge. "Come away," he muttered urgently, "come away." But Wande shook off his hand and waded around to the starboard side of the boat so that she could get a better look at the woman.

"Wande!" Mayr snapped, and she stopped in her tracks, not because her future husband's tone was imperative but because the look on the dead woman's face was one of abject horror. The unfortunate lady's blood must surely have turned to ice in her veins, for her death face was a scream of terror; the mouth open wide, grey lips pulled back in a shriek for mercy, and her eyes were also open, the viscera as black as pitch.

Wande hurriedly stepped away, becoming tangled in the reeds below the surface and plunging backwards into the water. Surfacing, she opened her mouth to cry out, then went under again. Once more she surfaced, this time choking and spluttering. Mayr grabbed hold of the front of her dress and yanked her roughly towards the bank, unceremoniously pushing her up onto the dirt below the willow, where she rolled out from under the shadows and sat coughing up water in the sunlight. Mayr joined her there and let her recover in her own time.

Wande shivered in spite of the warmth of the afternoon. "Is this the lady from the big house?"

"Aye," nodded Mayr, and he cast a look about, worried they might be overheard. "The faery lady."

Wande's eyes were wide. "But no-one on Shalott ever sees her. She never comes out."

"I've heard her though. My father has too. In the fields. In the morning and in the evening, you can hear her singing."

"Could hear her." Wande nodded her head at the barge hidden in the overgrowth. "What did she sing?"

"Holy songs, mournful songs." Mayr stood and pulled Wande to her feet. "We should get away from here. It doesn't feel like a nice place." Wande fell into step alongside Mayr, and they strode quickly down river, heading seaward towards the small cottage where Wande lived with her mother.

"We should let the elders know," Wande said.

"Leave it to me," Mayr said, "and let's not talk of it again."

Wande frowned but didn't retort. They walked in silence for a while, until Wande asked, "Why did she never come out?"

"They say she was cursed," answered Mayr, "now let's hear no more of it." And that was the end of the conversation.

Later that evening Wande paused as she washed the pots in the river, her eyes following the water upstream. She could just about make out the tributary, and the clump of willow trees that hid the barge from view, in the twilight. The lady had been travelling downstream to the sea, away from her big house. Wande knew the house. Indeed, everyone on Shalott was familiar with the house—set grandly in landscaped gardens, shining like a jewel among its neighbours.

Setting out on an adventure. How exciting that must have been. Oh to be that free!

Wande was only fifteen. She would be sixteen soon enough, and then she would be married to Mayr. There would be a baby before she was seventeen. She would have no adventures. She would be dutiful and caring, a wife and a mother, and she would die of boredom and childbearing before she was thirty. Probably. It was an excruciating thought.

How old had the lady been, Wande wondered. And who had cursed her, if Mayr spoke true?

Wande thought to ask her mother, but her mother was a practical woman, much given to common sense and action and not at all to fantasies and daydreams. She would not entertain fanciful discussion about curses and the like and was liable to give Wande a thick ear instead.

Wande carried the pots and dishes into the cottage, stowed them away, and lay down on her mattress. Sleep, when it came, was fleeting.

Sometime after two in the morning, a restless Wande rose and slipped outside. The moon was high and bright, a natural lighthouse, illuminating the landscape, and to her far left it lent its glittering reflection to the tops of the waves as the tide reversed and headed inland.

There was little sea-bound traffic at this time of night, but Wande's attention was drawn to a barge, sailing against the tide, down the river towards her. Its silk sails billowed proudly with no breeze to speak of, yet nothing else led the barge: No ghostly horses or oxen. Unnerved, Wande observed the approach of the boat, gleaming in the moonlight, something ethereal and otherworldly. The sound of singing drifted towards Wande. A song so sad and lonesome it would break your heart if you dallied to listen for too long.

Wande was enraptured by the apparition and the song, and she leaned precariously over the water's edge to peer more closely as the barge floated serenely by. The occupant reclined against her pillows, replete in her sumptuous gown. Her face, pale in the moonlight, cast down as she sang. It was a melancholic and beautiful sight to behold, but when the lady lifted her chin and glanced Wande's way, Wande shuddered in revulsion. The lady's eyes were gone.

Terrified, Wande ran into the cottage and closed and bolted the door. Jumping into bed, she pulled the cover up over her head, jammed her hands over her ears, and scrunched up her eyelids. Could she catch the woman's affliction simply by gazing upon it? Was that not how it was with the leprosy? Her mother had warned her of that.

Trembling, she remained hidden in her bed until the sun

had risen high in the sky, and her mother threatened to beat her if she didn't attend to her chores.

⁓

Wande tried to carry on with life as normal, but Mayr had not told anyone of the discovery of the barge in spite of saying he would do so, and Wande could not rid her mind of the image of the lady, hidden by circumstance and rotting underneath the weeping willows in the tributary, nor lose the memory of the ghost on the water. Neither could she understand why the lady was not missed. Surely, someone knew she was no longer resident in her house.

So it was, two days after the discovery of the barge, that Wande decided to head for the lady's house. She had no plan or mission beyond a quick walk. Wande merely wished to investigate where the woman had lived and whether she had a family. She was curious, and it was a way for her to have a small adventure on a day when she otherwise had little to keep her busy.

It was a hot day. Wande kicked up the red dust of the earth as she walked along the well-trodden path from her cottage towards Mayr's farm, past the tributary and the weeping willows and the wood that stretched out along this side of the river. She paused at the copse of trees and considered ducking her head underneath to gaze upon the lady's body once more, but the thought of the vacuous, viscous evilness of those eyes held Wande in check. Shuddering, she moved away, picking up her pace, heading for town.

Town was usually busy, and Wande enjoyed watching the merchants in their gaily-coloured robes and the market girls in their red cloaks, but today was the Sabbath and town was quiet. Wande walked purposefully on until she came to the settlement where the wealthier inhabitants of Shalott resided.

The houses and palaces here stood in their own grounds, decorated in the Moorish style with arched windows and tiles, gilt and beading. They quite took Wande's breath away. Apart from one.

It stood alone, huge and simple, comprising four grey walls and four grey towers in perfect symmetry. The windows were undecorated but gazed out over the most sumptuous of gardens and the river, flowing beyond. Wande dallied at the gates and gawked in admiration at the flower beds, bushes, and ornamental trees and fountains. Surely all of this beauty was the work of a team of talented gardeners.

In her excitement, Wande leant on a gate and was taken aback to find they were not locked. Without thinking, she stepped into the grounds and pulled the gate closed behind her. The audible sound of the iron gate's stern clunking gave her pause. She turned and rattled the bars, but the gate was firmly locked and would not open without a key.

Doubt began to creep into Wande's mind for the first time. What was she thinking? She was trespassing. Now she would need to find a member of the household and explain why she was in the grounds and beg for forgiveness—and release. She had heard rumours of burglars and the like being hung in the marketplace, or at least publicly whipped. She hoped that she would find a sympathetic ear.

Fearing the worst, Wande followed the paths that wound their way around the neat garden. She found herself at the rear of the house among a number of outbuildings, including a glass house for cultivating rare and exotic plants and a shed containing garden tools. The doors stood ajar, but alas, there was no sign of any member of the household. After hunting exhaustively for some time, Wande could only conclude that the lady of the house had not employed a staff, or they had all deserted the house after she had failed to return from her jaunt. Wande was left with no alternative but to approach the main entrance to make enquiries there.

The front door gaped open. She could have walked straight in, but discretion seemed the better part of valour and she elected to pull the bell instead. She yanked the cord and listened to the jangling of the bell reverberate around the large grey fortress of a house. She waited for slow and heavy footsteps to approach the door, but nobody came. It seemed she was entirely on her own.

Wande poked her head around the heavy front door and gazed into the expansive hallway. While the house from the outside was utilitarian and forbidding, the interior was completely the opposite. Complex tiling spread across the floor, and lavish wall-hangings covered every vertical surface. Stepping into the house with a gasp, Wande caught sight of the drawing room to her left. Elaborately-carved furniture graced the room, and a fire burned merrily in the grate.

The sweeping curve of the staircase invited Wande to gaze upwards to a glass dome far above her head, looking up and out at the brilliant blue of the sky. Wande placed her hand on the newel and then smoothed the wood of the banister. She followed her hand as it led her up, step by step, until she found herself on the first landing. She peered down at the hallway below, observing as the front door swung close by itself. She heard the distinct click of a lock.

Her breath caught in her throat. "Who's there?" she called, her voice wavering. "Hello?" She was answered only by her echo. Half sick of shadows, she had no choice but to go on.

There were several rooms on this landing, including a number of bedrooms. All of them were as exquisite as the drawing room below, but they remained empty and quiet, cold without the benefit of fires in grates. Wande ascended the final staircase and found herself in the lady's suite of rooms.

The first room was a bedroom, decorated with clean, white linen, the walls hung with the finest thick paper, delicately hand-painted with small blue and yellow flowers. An urn of fresh water stood beside a bowl awaiting use. Wande glanced down at her dusty hands in shame. She poured the sparkling water into the bowl and dipped her hands in. It felt good. She washed her face too, and considered her feet, but decided that was taking the hospitality the house was offering her a step too far. She dried her hands and face off on the thick white linen that was neatly folded nearby, grimacing as she stained it with the residue of red dust from the river bank.

The main room on this floor faced the river. Standing in the doorway, Wande could see a succession of barges heading towards Shalott. Some contained goods and were plain and functional; dirty, even. Others contained people, perhaps royalty. They were hung with sumptuous sails and decorated in bright colours. Wande thought again of the lady, lying in despair and decay beneath the weeping willows a few miles downstream.

This had been her house. Had she found it a place of

security and happiness? Wande wasn't sure about that. It felt at once welcoming but dark and secretive. It was too quiet by far.

Wande wandered into the main room. Yet again, the room had been decorated with great care. The soft furnishings and upholstery in various shades of green blended effortlessly together, creating a sense of the woods downstream. A large mirror dominated the back wall, set over a wide table, with a comfortable chair positioned in front. The lady must have sat here to work, Wande decided. There were books to read, a pile of embroidery and silks, and a small tapestry loom.

Refreshments had been neatly laid out on a small side table. They were fresh, delicate sandwiches and tiny cakes, perfectly-iced, minute things that could be eaten with one bite. Wande realised she was hungry. Would anyone miss a few of these exquisite little dainties? It was a shame to waste them. Selecting a triangle of bread, she held it to her lips and nibbled. The sea exploded on her tongue in a taste sensation, fresh and salty. Stunned, she picked a small yellow cake and cooed as sun-ripened mango tantalised her taste buds. Wande worked her way through the selection of goodies; sweet strawberries and perfect plum alternated with wood-smoked ham and cheddar with crunchy apple. Wande mopped the plates with her finger, cleaning every crumb.

It had been a long morning and post-lunch fatigue was threatening to set in. Wande perched on the chair in front of the mirror. She picked one of the books from the table, even though she couldn't read, and skimmed the pages. The light here was good, reflected from the window. When she looked up, she found she could watch the world go by on the river outside without turning around.

Glancing up into the corner of the mirror she spotted a large, black spider, busily spinning its web. Wande was surprised to see it there, given that the rest of the house was unnaturally spick and span. She watched it for some time, feeling lazy and full of lunch, entranced by its quick, precise movements, its legs working independently, and yet in unison, to create a trap of perfect symmetry and beauty. Wande pitied its prey.

Wande lost awareness of the time as she watched the busy spider. The sky in the mirror turned from a bright, unblemished, blue to a lighter turquoise hue, then burst into exuberant peach and lavender pastel shades as the sun fell into the sea. Was it her imagination, or a trick of the light? The spider pulsated with a vibrant energy, its body swelling, becoming ever more sleek and shiny. The hairs on its legs lengthening, its eyes wide and bright and so deeply black ...

Wande must have dozed because she started in alarm at the sound of something falling to the floor, quickly followed by a soft rustling. The book she had been looking through had fallen from the desk, and had been swiftly followed to the ground by the spider.

But not the spider.

Or rather it was the spider, but it was now something that was not quite spider and not quite human. Whatever it was had a woman's body, with the correct number of arms and legs, but its limbs were angular, its features pointed. The eyes—just two—were bulbous and dark, the nose neat and tidy. The woman's hair was coarse and had a life of its own—reaching towards Wande's reflection in the mirror. This aberration of a woman, dressed entirely in black, stood at Wande's side, glaring at her via the mirror. Wande stared back in horror and tried to rise.

The woman whipped her arm out and pinned Wande to the chair. Her mouth opened to reveal needle-like fangs. "Sssssssssstay!" she hissed, and Wande cowered under the woman's touch, the reality of her adventure and the consequences she was likely to face beginning to make themselves apparent. Wande was doomed.

"What do you want from me?" she shrieked.

The woman's mouth drew back in some semblance of a smile, the tips of her fangs glistening with spittle. "You have been drawn to me, little Wande, since you found the girl on the barge." She elongated every sibilant with an undisguised relish.

"The ... the lady?"

"No, no. She was no lady. She was my maidservant. I sent her down river, and she failed me. The fact is, I have a task unfinished."

Wande shuddered and wept. "Please don't hurt me," she begged.

"Shhh, sweet one. It is a simple enough job for one as beautiful as you, so young, so virtuous." The woman sighed theatrically. "Yes, so innocent, and yet you dared to enter my garden and my house. You sit in my chair having consumed the delectations freshly prepared in my kitchen. In my benevolence, I have spared your life. You owe me, and it is but a simple recompense."

Wande nodded, frightened enough that she would have agreed to commit murder on the woman's behalf if so instructed.

"Come little one," the woman said and held out one of her elongated limbs, indicating the stairs. Wande drew herself up, self-conscious in her worn gown, speckled with the remnants of her lunch. She carefully made her way down the stairs, her legs heavy as lead.

The unlikely pair stepped out into the twilight and made their way down to the river. A barge lay tethered to the bank, fully-rigged with a glorious array of silk sails, and cushions spread across the deck.

The woman handed Wande into the barge. "Make yourself at home, little one," she instructed. "The tide is going out. I need you to lie in the barge and drift all the way down the river, through the woods to the sea. To Camelot. I have a gift for those that abide there."

Wande felt hope. With any luck she could steer the boat towards the riverbank as she sailed past her cottage. If that wasn't possible, she could jump into the water and swim to the side. She was a good swimmer. And if the worst came to the worst? Why she could hand the gift over at Camelot, explain what had happened, and return home after any ensuing furore had died down. She would be free of this nightmare yet. "What is the gift?" asked Wande, settling herself back on the cushions and looking around the barge. She could see no box or package.

The woman reached a taut angular limb out to Wande, the end sharp and deadly. She punctured the skin on Wande's neck, quickly and precisely, and drew the limb back almost apologetically.

Wande drew her breath in sharply and clamped her hand to her neck. When she drew the hand away, dark blood filled the creases of her palm.

"You see, I sent my maid a few days ago, but her barge sailed too close to land, and became snarled in the trees. I won't make that mistake twice. Sleep soundly, sweet Wande. Pleasant journey."

"Wait!" cried Wande.

The woman gestured at the barge. In one majestic movement it moved out into the centre of the river as though manoeuvred by a team of invisible oarsmen. It ran with the tide, the sails billowing overhead.

"What have you done to me?" shrieked Wande.

"It is a plague. You are the carrier of my gift to Camelot, dear child. But don't worry, it is fast acting and only momentarily painful."

Frantically, Wande attempted to stand, intending to throw herself from the boat, swim to the riverside and seek help, but her legs would not obey the impulses sent from her brain. The first spasm rocked her body. Her back arched, and she vomited. When it passed, all her strength ebbed away, and she fell back on the cushions. The barge was picking up speed now, and as Wande turned her head, she spotted the tributary and weeping willows where the maid had met her own fate.

Wande barely had the energy to weep, but a few fat tears escaped from her eyelids as she passed her own cottage. She turned her head, wishing to see her mother one last time as another convulsion tore through her. The pain was excruciating: a million needles puncturing her internal organs. She opened her mouth to scream in agony, her lips pulling back against her teeth, and the scream caught in her throat as the blood that had coursed so warmly through her veins froze, and her eyes, full of toxins, burst with thick black blood.

She died that way, and the boat drifted on, dead-pale beneath the houses high above the bank, gleaming under the moonlit sky. On she went, into the mist, past the waning woods towards the sea where Camelot nestled on the headland.

Silent into Camelot,
Out upon the wharfs they came,
Knight and burger, lord and dame,
And around the prow they read her name,
The Lady of Shalott.
Who is this? And what is here?
And in the lighted palace near
Died the sound of royal cheer;
And they cross'd themselves for fear...

*With additional material by Lord Alfred Tennyson

Fragile Hearts

Charlie Haynes

On the wildest part of the Western cliffs, a small nook in the landscape sheltered a small town; protected from the worst of the sea by a harbour wall. Skeletal remains of a once-vibrant fishing fleet clanked in their chains as they crumbled inch by inch into the sea, and the old train line that brought holiday-makers to the seaside and took the fish to market had long since been covered in brambles. The town centre, once cheerful and bustling, was the kind of boarded-up place people hurried through after dark as they avoided catching the eyes of young men scrawling graffiti with the unhurried, bored arrogance of teenagers.

Adelaide lived half-way up the southerly hill in a comfortable house facing the sea, which her family had lived in for three generations. Kyra lived across the river in a two-bedroom flat above an empty shop with a harassed mother and three sisters, so it wasn't surprising that they hadn't met until they were put in the same class at school.

Perhaps in another story they would have hated each other, the cherished girl who knew no discomfort and the spiky, resentful tomboy. As it was though, on the first day of school, Adelaide saw Kyra sitting at a bench alone at lunch, not eating. She sat down and gave her a sandwich without saying a word, and just like that, they were friends.

Not just friends, best friends. Others thought it odd, and even Kyra sometimes wondered why Adelaide liked her when the other kids, and even some of the adults, avoided her and whispered behind her back. She knew they did this because she could hear them, and she could hear them because she had cast a spell allowing her to do so, and she could do this because Kyra was a sorcerer.

She didn't know where her abilities came from—perhaps from the father who had vanished before she was born; her sisters, after all, each had a different father and none of them could do what she could. All she knew was that she could do things to people, and that learning to do things to people was far more interesting than trying to make them like her when they seemed so determined not to. Not that it mattered. She had seen into people's minds and didn't much like what was in most of them.

Adelaide was not a sorcerer. She had no powers of her own, not a single magical bone in her body, but she had her own unique ability. She had a voice more beautiful than the birds in the trees, a voice that could transport a person in time and give hope back to those who had lost theirs. Adelaide's voice could make sunlight stand still. She was not beautiful or particularly clever, but she was kind and sweet, and she had chosen Kyra.

She remained a calming influence on Kyra as they grew, and Kyra began to stretch the boundaries of her powers. She discovered she wasn't just a simple hedgerow witch who brewed herbal potions and chanted spells that didn't work. Kyra could make the moon disappear or a storm rise. She could make frogs pour out of people's pockets. It was remarkable how often that happened in the super-market before the manager assigned Kyra to the stock room. She didn't mind.

Sorcerer. She held tight onto the word. She was special, and Adelaide could see it, even if nobody else could.

As they approached adulthood, Adelaide's parents worried about what the girls would do with hardly any jobs in town. They worried about Adelaide spending too much time with Kyra and wasting her potential. Kyra's mother mostly worried about earning enough to feed her daughters. She didn't have much energy to spare for Kyra's troubles, and it was a relief for her when the friends moved in together, to a ramshackle little house right at the top of the other hill. It was cheap enough for the girls to afford with their meagre pub and supermarket wages, it kept them warm and dry, and they were happy there, for a time at least.

Then Huw came along.

Huw had left school a couple of years before the girls. He was tall and dreamy, he played rugby and sang in the choir—he had even gone away to university in the big city. He was on a trip home just after graduating when he heard Adelaide's voice from the path as she collected shells on the foreshore, and he fell instantly, hopelessly in love with her.

Adelaide was delighted, but Kyra found herself unable to feel the joy she should for her friend. How could Adelaide, who might be wonderful but who was undoubtedly plainer than Kyra, capture this good, handsome man just by singing, while the local boys all avoided her at the same time as they spread rumours about the kind of girl she was? It wasn't fair.

Huw, however, seemed different from the others. He was sweet to Adelaide, making sure she got home safely and kissing her gently on the doorstep as Kyra watched from a darkened upstairs window. It was months before he stayed over, first on the sofa then eventually in Adelaide's room at her suggestion.

Kyra became obsessed. She stalked Huw online and looked into his mind, even after Adelaide asked her not to. She hung about the house hoping to catch a glimpse of him or exchange a snippet of conversation, and spent so much time mooning at work that she almost lost her job. She made passes at him when they were all drunk and Adelaide had fallen asleep, but to no avail. Huw and Adelaide sang together as they cooked and laughed together in the garden and snuggled up on the sofa together, and he looked at Adelaide with such love that Kyra's insides boiled.

Then Kyra was fired from her job after an incident with a customer who was almost buried under an avalanche of ketchup and soy sauce bottles. After the hospital eventually worked out what was food and what was blood, he needed twelve stitches. Nobody could say she had touched him, but she was fired nonetheless.

Kyra stormed home. How was this fair? More importantly, what was she going to do now? She wanted to talk, to feel Adelaide's soothing hand stroke her head in the dark, to have Adelaide tell her everything would be okay. But when she got home, Adelaide and Huw were in the kitchen together. Adelaide listened and made sympathetic noises, but her attention was only half there. Huw told her she should go back in the next day and speak to the manager, that she should speak to Citizen's Advice, that she should get her CV together and he could pass it to a few people. He shelled out practical advice until she wanted to scream.

A storm gathered itself around Kyra's rage, the worst storm the town had seen in fifty years. It whipped the town for a night and a day, and lightning hit the old house on the hill twice. In the middle of the storm, just as people were struggling to get to work or school against the wind, some of townspeople saw Adelaide walking down the hill in the half-light, all alone. She looked eerie, lit from within, with white-blonde hair flying around her head. She passed straight through town to the harbour, upright and blank-eyed, oblivious to the wind and rain.

It was these eyewitnesses that—rather reluctantly—saved Kyra from jail, because nobody saw Adelaide or Huw after that morning. The butcher and the coffee shop owner both saw Adelaide pass, and they saw Huw not ten minutes later, racing out towards the harbour after her. They had good positions and were watching the storm, and neither saw Kyra. A small boy swore he saw the light on in Kyra's room and her moving about, and though people wanted to believe she had something to do with the disappearance, they had to admit that in the face of the evidence it seemed unlikely.

Nobody, not the butcher or the coffee shop owner or even the postman buffeted by the wind, saw what happened to Huw and Adelaide. One moment they were there, the next they were gone. The witnesses all said that they assumed at the time they had taken shelter in one of the old sea-caves. They hadn't noticed.

A few minutes after Huw ran to the sea though, a tiny bird took off from the harbour wall. None of the witnesses noticed it in the storm. Why would they? But it was there nonetheless, and it flew straight up the hill toward the old house as though there were no wind at all, as though it were being drawn on a string.

Kyra was distraught when neither Huw nor Adelaide returned. She was called in for questioning. The police searched the house two times, three times. Had Adelaide and Huw argued, they asked? No, she cried, they seemed very much in love. Eventually the police left her with a warning not to leave town and a follow-up visit from a singularly unsympathetic family liaison officer.

Was it a double suicide? But why no note? A crime of passion? Perhaps Huw discovered Adelaide with another man and pushed her over the edge, accidentally toppling in too? Or vice versa? Where were the bodies though, why had they not washed up? Gossip swirled and eddied around the town, new waves breaking every few days with the next police update, but there was never any news to report, never a body. Then Adelaide's perfect little sister became pregnant at fifteen, and the gossips mostly moved on.

Without Adelaide to share the rent, and with no job, Kyra couldn't keep the house for long before her meagre savings ran out. The morning after the electricity was cut off she moved out, just as dawn broke. She was wearing her old coat with an even older blanket wrapped over the top, and she carried a single bag containing clothes, a sleeping bag and one plate and a saucepan.

If anybody had been around to see her, they might have noticed what looked like a small bird sitting on her shoulder. If anybody had wished to get close enough to greet her, which they wouldn't have done, they would have seen that the bird was a tiny mistle thrush with a fine silver chain around its leg that ended in Kyra's pocket.

Over the far side of the hill and set back across a number of fields was a patch of ancient yew woodland. It was a long walk from town, and it was rumoured that the site had been mined until a rockfall killed most of the workers. It was damp and cold in the lee of the old quarry face and nothing else grew in the unnatural quiet of the gloomy trees, so people avoided the place.

Kyra was not afraid of the woods. Unnatural things resided there, certainly, some that she had put there herself. If the ghosts of miners resided there, they were the ones that should be wary.

In the centre of the woods stood a small tumbledown cottage that she had found as a child. It had been her sanctuary for years, the place she came to practice and store things she didn't want even Adelaide to see, lest she think badly of Kyra. The yew next to it was old and twisted, with papery bark and deep green leaves that let no sun touch the ground. This place would provide her with shelter and protection from the townspeople. She needed nobody else, she thought, stroking the bird as she fastened its chain to the tree.

And there she lived for a while in peace. She foraged for berries and mushrooms and sat in the low boughs of the tree as she talked to the mistle thrush, who sang wistful tunes in return. They were together at last, she told him, just like she'd always wanted. Just like they'd always wanted. The silver chain remained attached to Huw's leg though, just long enough to stretch his wings but not far enough to be free.

Every day she walked an hour to the clifftop a little way outside the town, and she sat next to the derelict lighthouse and searched the glittering sea. Every day she trudged home in the evening tired and hungry and disappointed, until one day under a heavy sky, there was a flash of something on the rocks below. Kyra found herself staring into the enormous round black eyes of an Adelaide who didn't recognise her. This new Adelaide looked away and sank her pointed teeth into a dead fish. She ripped it to shreds and ate it with relish, bones and all, then she rolled off the rock. With a flip of a tail that was the same grey-green as the ocean itself, she was gone.

"I saw her," Kyra reported to Huw when she got home. She was triumphant. He chirruped and strained at the length of his silver chain, and she laughed.

"There's no point. She won't even know you now she's mer. Her heart is as cold as the sea and she lives in the depths of the ocean. What could she possibly want with you now? You can't survive out there—you could barely make it to town and back poor thing." She stroked his beak. "It's just you and me now. Don't worry, I'll look after you. We can be happy here together."

But they were not happy there together. A cold, hard winter passed. Huw sang more sadly each day, and Kyra became bitter. Why could he not be content with her? And she was not doing so very well either: She had no appetite and wasted away, both in person and in power. Even the thought of playing jokes on people she hated using her powers left her feeling dry as dust, and she shrank inside herself.

On the first day when it felt like spring again, she walked out to the little clifftop, just as she had done every day, and she sat wrapped in her old blanket to stare at the sea, just as she did every day.

She hardly knew what she was doing, only that she ached inside and that watching the sea was the only thing left that soothed her soul, that this routine was all that held her together. The sea was as flat and dull as her insides, and she listened to the rush of water on the rocks and let her mind drift into blankness.

Then something that didn't belong caught her eye. Adelaide was back.

It was an even stranger version of Adelaide than before—wild-looking and fierce with her golden hair turned to seaweed—but it was unmistakably her.

And Kyra knew. She knew why she came here every day and why she ached inside. She'd had it all wrong, the jealousy and the hate and wishing she could steal Huw from Adelaide. Because it was never Huw she wanted for herself. It was Adelaide.

For a brief moment Kyra felt like the sun had come out, and she was filled with hope. She stood, ready to wave and to call Adelaide's name. They would be together again. But then she put her arms down again and stared at the hands that had cast an unbreakable curse. Adelaide could not live on the land any more, and Kyra could not live on the sea. Even if she could undo the curse, which she didn't think was possible for she had cast it well, she was too weak now. Her powers had run out of her like sand through a broken hourglass. Adelaide was mer now, and her kind-hearted friend was gone.

Kyra watched until Adelaide dove back into the slate folds of the sea, then walked back to her home in the woods. Huw was singing. How sad he sounded. The song was suddenly unbearable to her, a reminder of what she could not have.

She walked up to the old yew and took the silver chain off his leg. He watched her with his head on one side, and she stamped her feet and shooed him.

"Get out!" she shouted, and there was a flurry of wings as every other bird in the clearing took fright. She couldn't stand to be near him a second longer. "Get out, get out, get out!"

He launched himself off the branch, wobbly from lack of practise, and seconds later his shadow was lost in the trees. Kyra sat on the forest floor, rolled herself in the blanket, and cried herself to sleep.

Huw flew up, up, up, high above the canopy. He wheeled

in the air then pointed his beak into the salty wind and flapped his wings.

It was almost sunset by the time he arrived at the cliffs, but he flew low over the water, searching. There was no sign of Adelaide, and he was exhausted and hungry and close to giving up when he heard a familiar sound, one that lifted his heart with hope and washed away his weariness.

Adelaide had appeared on a rock in the shallows, singing, and her song was as pure and strong as ever. He flew down and circled her head, adding his harmony to hers.

She looked terrifying with her sharp fangs and inhuman eyes, but Huw gathered his courage and landed on the tip of her outstretched tail. If she could sing their song and remember him, she could not be wholly mer. The strength of her love had kept her heart warm in the cold ocean and she had come back for him. His own heart soared, and he almost burst with joy, swelling and ruffling his feathers as he saw in her eyes that she still recognised him.

Indeed, Adelaide did recognise Huw, but he was wrong. She had spent too long in the lonely dark, and though he knew that this was Huw, it meant nothing to her. She sang their sweet song until he trusted her, until he hopped closer and sat on her shoulder. Then, just as she had done with so many creatures before him, she caught her prey in her claws and smiled at him with shark-like teeth.

In the forest, Kyra tossed and turned in her blanket. Her heart raced, and she burned up despite the cold. When she woke in the night coughing, she thought she saw the skin of her arms flake like the bark of the yew, felt her insides crumble into nothing. She tried to draw her power around her, to hold herself together, but it was no good. In the morning, a bird landed and pecked at the blanket, but it contained nothing but dry leaves and an uncomfortable feeling that made the bird take flight again. The clearing lay quiet.

Adelaide felt Kyra's spirit leave, felt the curse snap. She might, perhaps, have been able to turn back now, but why would she want to? She was mer now, and the whole world below was hers. Adelaide left without looking back, and she sang a song that could pull stars from the sky as she swam deep into the ocean.

In the Light

Shanthi Sam

She had never looked more beautiful to him. In fact, he found he couldn't take his eyes off her. Her family fussed around; her mother adjusted the veil and glowed and clucked, her sisters fidgeted with the beading on the heavily-embroidered bodice and straightened the folds of the skirt. Her father stood beside her proudly, as if he had made her all by himself, idea and effort, the finished product his achievement. Or maybe it was just that he was paying for the wedding—sending his little girl off in style. A beach wedding, out in the open, with the sun shining on them, the sand damp under their bare feet. Her dream, on her special day. He beamed at them.

She met their eyes as they orbited her, pouring adoration back and forth. He wanted to step forward and stand beside her. Claim her as he would in only a few hours. He checked his watch. An hour and a half. It was creeping up fast. He'd been uncomfortable with doing the pictures before the wedding, seeing her in the dress. He knew his mother would have shaken her head, if she'd been here.

Bad luck, he could hear her sighing, bad luck...and then with her voice in his ear, he'd gone and ripped his shoe on the rocks, scrambling up and down at the photographer's ring-master commands. But now he was glad he'd agreed. Now the posing was behind them with just the wedding to go.

He didn't believe in luck, either way. He believed in committing and taking the good with the bad. Though his vows were much more flowery than that. He smiled to himself; she'd made sure of it—corrections in a red pen, though with the red heart and smiley face at the bottom, taking the sting off.

Again, he checked the urge to join them. It seemed almost intrusive to push his way into the family circle. He wasn't family yet, though all that would change soon enough. He'd be one of them. He thought he caught her brother's eye and half lifted a hand in a wave before he realized that he was looking at something else. He hoped he'd remembered the ring.

His own brother's absence was like a small stabbing pain. He'd always thought they'd be standing side-by-side on a day like this. The distance, the timing, the money... they couldn't accommodate everyone.

He checked his watch again. His friends would be turning up in a bit. They knew it'd be frowned upon if they came too early. After 11, she'd said firmly, and how could anyone argue? But it would have been nice to have the company as he waited, especially with his family so far away.

He leaned against the tree and looked down the beach. It was already quite warm. He'd worried about the weather, that it would rain. He had not foreseen this cloudless sky and the bright glare of the sun. He looked down the beach to the lighthouse at the tip of the far sweep of rock; its white height glistening, bleached in the light. At night, you could see the lighthouse lamp glittering across the bay, but in the sun the whole tower seemed to shine even brighter. A glow warding off danger, over the centuries, crying out its warning. Beware! The rocks!

A breath of cool air blew through the woods, calling him in. He stepped into the shade, hearing the laughter and bustle die almost instantly and be replaced by the alluring refrain of a bird. He took another few steps, tiny casuarina cones pricking at his feet, tickling rather than painful. He filled his lungs and felt the wedding nerves ease, every step a lightening of the band he'd felt around his head from the moment he'd woken up. Once he started, he kept going. Walk it off, he could hear his dad say, walk it off.

Almost an hour to go. He'd feel better for the exercise—blow the cobwebs and the nervous energy away. They wouldn't miss him. His stride lengthened. There was grass under his feet now, rough straggly sand grass. And from somewhere ahead of him the sound of traffic, sweeping softly through the trees. A few minutes later he was out of the woods and standing beside the road. It felt oddly surreal, a parallel life.

A car screeched to a halt just ahead of him, making him jump. The driver leaned over and hooked the passenger door open, calling out. "Need a lift, mate?" He nodded without thinking, the seat drawing him into its shelter, the door closing protectively as they started up.

"What's with the tux? You look like you're escaping from a wedding." The driver broke into a giggle, delighted at his own joke.

He smiled weakly.

"Where to, then?"

He finally found his voice, though it sounded strange, like someone else's voice, someone sitting next to him and quite separate. "Anywhere, please. I need to buy some shoes."

A New Beginning

Sarah Jeffery

Shona's skin starts to prickle as she stands on the edge of the crumbling cliff top, staring across the bay. She has no idea how long she has been there, as her watch is broken. The result of yet another fight with Tom. Usually time mattered, but not today. She's finally free. Dark grey clouds roll inland as the wind gets stronger. She can feel its chill around her neck; it's definitely going to take a while to get used to her new pixie crop. Tom would hate it, but it doesn't matter as he's never going to see it. There's no going back; too much has gone into this moment for her to change her mind now.

The old lighthouse glitters across the bay, its beacon guiding ships to safety. No-one should be sailing on a night like this; it's too dangerous. The North Sea is unpredictable at the best of times, but tonight it's wild. Waves crash on the rocks below, deafening the crying seagulls overhead. Despite the squally weather, Shona wishes she was out at sea. Nothing beats being out on the open water. It is the only place where she's free from Tom's grasp. The only place he isn't in control. That's why she hasn't sailed for so long. He won't let her; it isn't safe. But life with Tom isn't safe either.

She has the scars to prove it; some fainter than others, but each one tells a story. With the tip of her right index finger she traces the most recent one—along her fore-head—which is more visible due to her recent haircut. The sound of her head cracking on the kitchen bench will live with her forever. Shona had never seen Tom so angry, and all because of a stupid text message. It was totally innocent, but he wouldn't listen. Instead he assumed the worst, accused her of being unfaithful, calling her an 'ungrateful bitch' before lashing out. Next thing she remembers is coming round on her way to hospital with Tom crying beside her, pretending he had found her on the kitchen floor.

Her stomach churns as she remembers how he manipu-lated everyone into believing his version of events. There was no point in disagreeing. Shona had learnt that the hard way. Life was much simpler if you agreed with everything Tom said. Deep down she knew the hospital staff knew the truth; she could see it in their eyes. But she didn't want their pity; she needed their help although there was no way she could ask. Tom's mind games over the last five years had destroyed her. She is no longer an outgoing, confident young woman; instead she is like the broken wreck washed up on the shore below.

A sudden gust of wind catches her by surprise. Losing her footing she stumbles forward, nearly falling over the edge. One false move and she'll be gone. Shona anchors herself against the elements; there's no time for mistakes. Not tonight. She has to be strong. She can't let Tom win—not again. The air crackles with electricity as the bay lights up, making the hairs on her neck stand up like saluting soldiers. Her clothes are damp, clinging to her icy-cold skin. If she's not careful, she'll end up 'catching her death' as her Granny used to say, and she can't afford to be ill. She pulls her coat around her, trying to seek shelter. It's no good; the storm is only beginning. Shona's eyes sting, but she's not sure if it's her new coloured contacts or the sea salt in the air. Water drips off the end of her nose, splashing her sodden canvas shoes. She wipes away her tears with her sleeve, smearing her make-up even further, before stepping closer to the edge. Shona needs to act fast before it's too late. She can't risk being found, not when she's come this far. There's no going back—not if she wants to stay alive. This is her only option; it's now or never.

In the beginning, life with Tom had been perfect. He was everything Shona wanted—caring, loving, attentive. He made her feel like a princess. But everything changed five years ago, on their second anniversary.

"Close your eyes," Tom said as she got into his old battered VW camper van, "and no peeking."

"What's going on?"

"Shh, you'll find out soon."

Shona felt Tom lean in through the passenger door. "What are you doing?"

"I know what you're like, so just going to make sure you don't cheat," said Tom as he tied a scarf over Shona's eyes.

Shona started to panic. Tom had been acting weird lately, and she couldn't quite put her finger on the reason behind it.

"You'll not be disappointed. Now sit back and relax. We'll be there shortly."

Shona couldn't relax; she hated being kept in the dark. She listened carefully for any clues to where they were going, but Tom read her mind and turned on the radio, blocking out any outside noise. After a short drive the camper van stopped. Tom opened his door Shona caught a faint whiff of a familiar smell—seaweed. They were at the beach. Tom insisted she remained blindfolded for a few more minutes as he guided her to their final destination.

After a ten-minute walk he untied her blindfold, and whispered "Surprise" into her left ear. His breath made her shiver despite the warmth of the glorious sunshine. Looking back she should have seen it as a sign, but at the time she was too overwhelmed by the picnic laid out in front of her.

"Wow, this is amazing. You've gone to so much trouble. Thank you."

Shona couldn't believe it. Tom had never done anything like this before. It was so over the top for their two-year anniversary, but she ignored the alarm bells that started to ring at the back of her mind. Tom had thought of everything: he'd prepared all of her favourite foods and chosen her favourite coastal spot for their celebratory picnic. She loved being by the sea; it was perfect.

Tom popped open the Champagne, laughing as the cork narrowly missed a flock of hungry seagulls who were eyeing up their spread.

"Thanks for a great two years," Shona said, clinking glasses with him.

He smiled, not saying anything as he watched Shona take her first sip. Tom didn't have to wait long. Shona gasped as something glittery caught her eye at the bottom of her glass.

"Will you marry me?" Tom asked.

Caught up in the moment, Shona said, "Yes."

If only she'd known how much her life would change by agreeing to become Mrs Bradbury, she would have never married Tom. Within weeks he had persuaded her to move in with him, and that's when the mind games began. She didn't see it at first, despite her friends' best attempts of warning her. Tom slowly took over her life. By the time they got married, he had changed the way she looked, convinced her she didn't need to work, and persuaded her that she no longer needed her friends.

Shona misses her best friend, Jenny. She considered contacting her, but after so long it was too difficult to pick up the phone. Jenny had been right about Tom. She had seen the warning signs, unlike Shona. If only she had listened, things might have been different. Jenny would have helped her, but Shona pushed her away, believing Tom's opinion that she was a bad influence, when it was the other way around. In the end, Jenny gave up trying to convince Shona to leave and she walked away.

Standing on the cliff top, Shona wishes she could turn back the clock. She should have left with Jenny, that cold November day two years ago. They met at a seaside cafe, away from prying eyes as Shona didn't want Tom to know she was meeting her best friend of fifteen years. She also knew how Jenny would react when she saw her—and she was right.

"Bloody hell, what have you done?"

"Don't Jenny, please. You'll get used it."

"Christ, if I hadn't recognised your awful coat I would have walked straight past you."

Shona knew she should have warned Jenny, but she'd forgotten. She'd been too worried about doing the washing, the ironing, cleaning the house and preparing tea. Making sure everything at home was perfect.

"Don't you like it?"

"No, it doesn't suit you. Why blonde?"

Before Shona could answer, Jenny said, "I assume it wasn't your idea, and is yet another part of Tom's transformation."

"Jenny please, you're over-exaggerating. I needed a change, that's all. I don't want to fall out."

"Sorry. He's far too controlling though and you've changed so much—new look, new hair—what's next?"

"That's not fair. Things are just different."

"You mean you're different, now." Jenny said, reaching across the table.

Shona flinched before Jenny could touch her. She was in agony from last night's fight; her wrists throbbed from Tom pinning her down and her body was bruised all over. She tugged the sleeves of her coat, attempting to hide the evidence. She wasn't quick enough. Jenny's hawk-eyes didn't miss a thing.

"Oh Shona, not again."

Shona stayed silent, knowing if she answered the floodgates would open. She couldn't get upset in public; Tom said crying was a sign of weakness.

"I thought things had changed when you gave up work." Jenny said.

If only, Shona thought. She'd hoped the beatings would stop once Tom had her at home full-time, but they'd increased. The slightest thing set him off; she could no longer gauge his moods. Life with Tom was frightening.

Shona shook her head and said, "Not really."

"Why didn't you tell me? You can't go on like this, you have to leave him, Shona."

"I can't. I love him and he loves me."

"No he doesn't. If Tom truly loved you he wouldn't beat you up."

"He doesn't mean to; he's just so busy and stressed—"

"That's not an excuse to use you as a punch bag. You should report him."

"No way. It will make everything worse."

"Shona! He's dangerous. Why can't you see that? He'll never stop and one day it'll be over."

"Don't be ridiculous."

"I'm not. I'm telling the truth. You need to get out now before it's too late."

Shona sighed, Jenny just didn't understand. It wasn't as simple as just walking out, she'd never be free from Tom. He would never let her go.

"I'm sorry Jenny, but I can't just up and leave. Tom needs me."

"This is no good. I'm never going to persuade you to go," Jenny said, choking back tears. "I can't do this anymore. I can't watch you let him destroy you."

If only Shona had listened, the past two years could have been totally different.

Shona still couldn't believe how stupid she had been. Tom had manipulated her for far too long. He had moulded her like an artist building a clay model. He had shaped her to perfection, but it wasn't enough. He became increasingly frustrated, and his outbursts intensified. There was no need for Tom to try and break her, she was already broken.

A clap of thunder reverberates around the bay, bouncing off the cliffs as Shona watches a boat trying to navigate the end of the south pier. The weather is getting worse; she couldn't have picked a better day to shed her past. Stepping out of her wet shoes, she feels the ground squelching between her toes. She unzips her rucksack and carefully removes a smaller bag, checking its contents. Everything she needs is inside. It's finally time to say goodbye. As she drops the rucksack beside her shoes, a searing pain jolts up her left arm reminding her why she's about to disappear. Yet another injury that hadn't healed properly—her body couldn't take anymore. Tom would never change. After years of broken promises she had finally realised it wasn't her, it was him.

She needed fixing and her only chance to heal was to be Tom-free. Shona knew it wouldn't be easy, as she'd tried before. This time was different though—she was stronger. Tom was in for a shock when he returned from his business trip. His dutiful wife would not be there to welcome him. He would see her carefully-worded note. He'd never see Shona again.

Shona takes one last look around her before taking a deep breath and stepping forward. Teetering on the cliff edge feels liberating, and she wonders what it must feel like to fly. One more step and she'll experience it for herself. But there isn't time. The storm will soon be over, and she needs to cover her tracks. Leaving the contents of her old life behind in her rucksack, she wipes her muddy feet on her fleece and steps into her trainers before throwing the bag over the edge. She has to make it look convincing, she needs Tom to believe she's gone.

Shona steps onto the safety of the rocky pathway—heads towards the woods; knowing that it isn't really the end, it's just the beginning.

Different Memory, Same Outcome

Julie Archer

Issy Meyer sat on the shoreline and exhaled as an air of calm finally settled around her.

The gentle sound of the water lapping on the sand soothed her as she, once again, reflected how she had got there. A whirlwind proposal had swept her off her feet, but three months into the engagement she had discovered her so-called fiancé in a compromising position with one of the receptionists from his office. And it hadn't been the first occasion by all accounts. She was tired of feeling second best, despite the ring on her finger, and this time she had promptly dumped him and run away to the seaside. It helped that her oldest friend in the world wanted someone to assist in opening her coffee-shop-cum-art-gallery, the grandly named The Woods &The Sea. Coffee and art were two things Issy definitely knew something about. It hadn't been a hard decision for her to throw in her job as an assistant at a gallery in London, although she knew she would miss being located next to an independent coffee shop that brewed the most glorious-tasting java she had ever experienced. But the opportunity to decamp to a delightfully-touristy part of South West England was the perfect escape. It was somewhere she wouldn't be faced with hideous reminders of what might have been. The Woods &The Sea was set in an unspoilt, sheltered bay amongst evergreens and pines. Issy thought that the name was apt. It certainly fulfilled the 'sea' part, although the 'woods' felt a little tenuous as the car park was only backed by a couple of rows of trees, hardly enough to constitute the true meaning of the word.

She heard Helen call her name and threw the remains of her cold coffee onto the sand. She dusted off the backs of her jeans—no need for a designer label in these parts—and strolled back up to the cafe. She carefully made her way past the builders who were putting the finishing touches onto the new counter, creating lots of dust and finding interesting new swear words to use when things went wrong. Helen was waiting for her at a table in the one corner of the cafe that had actually been finished.

"Right," Helen said. She pointed to the piles of large unopened envelopes, flyers, business cards and the odd portfolio. "That lot came in response to my open call to local artists and photographers who would be interested in selling their work here. As I have about as much artistic nous as that table, your job is to go through and select some stuff that's going to sell. Remember, there will be a lot of tourists and second-home-owners popping in, so I guess anything that reminds them of what a fantastic time they had here would work!"

Issy laughed. "You don't need me then, if that's your criteria."

"Ah, but I don't know what's good. I just know what I like."

"By the sounds of it, that's exactly what your punters will be saying."

"I'll make you a coffee, just get on with it!"

As Helen busied herself making the coffee, Issy looked gratefully at her. Helen had been the first person she had turned to when she had found out about Joel's infidelity. When she had suggested Issy help with The Woods &The Sea, it made perfect sense. Issy was living rent free with Helen in her cute, two-bedroom chocolate box cottage just a stone's throw away from the cafe. They spent the days sorting out menus, table plans, and staff rotas and the evenings drinking wine, eating ready meals or takeaway, and gossiping about men. Helen classed herself as between boyfriends, which basically meant she was seeing as many men as were interested in her. And of course, Issy was 'in recovery'. Finding someone else was the last thing on her mind.

Helen set a mug down beside her, and Issy realised it was time to get to work. She pulled her long, dark hair up into a ponytail and started sorting through the collection in front of her. She rearranged the big pile into three further piles—ones she really liked, ones she wasn't sure about, and ones that were definitely not right. The ones she considered ripe for sale were those featuring local landscapes and seascapes along with boats and even a few animals. They were classics and you couldn't really go wrong. Bearing in mind Helen's description of the potential clientele, this would be easy pickings for them.

She turned to one of the final sets of pictures and caught her breath. There, right in front of her, were a set of stunning photographs of Jersey's Corbiere lighthouse. She stared at the shots of the lighthouse, built on a rocky outcrop and only accessible by way of a causeway. Whoever had taken the photographs had cleverly captured it at different times of the day, from morning to evening. The lighthouse lamp glittered across the bay in the night-time frames. That image burned into Issy's brain. Joel knew that it was one of Issy's favourite places in the world and had taken her there one evening on a surprise break to the island. They had enjoyed a romantic picnic, watched the sun set over the horizon, and then Joel had proposed. It had been the most amazing moment of Issy's life so far, and she had fantasised about everything that was to come—marriage, children, a proper house, pets... An unexpected wave of nausea washed over her.

"Is this some kind of sick joke?" She jumped up from the table and waved the contact sheets in Helen's face.

Helen looked at her as if she didn't have a clue what Issy was talking about. "What's up?"

"This! Did Joel ask you to do this? How does he even know I'm here?"

"I have no idea what you're on about, what is this place?" Helen took a closer look at the photographs and her face fell as she recognised the location. "Oh."

"So when's he coming to make another apology about his dreadful behaviour? Why did you tell him I was here?"

"Issy, I haven't. I wouldn't do that! I don't think this has anything to do with Joel at all. Check out the contact info on the back."

Issy turned the picture over and there, in the bottom right hand corner, was a sticker with *Ben Hudson, Photographer* and all the ways you could get in touch with him. "Oh." Her word mirrored Helen's previous reaction.

Helen shook her head. "See? Nothing underhand or weird going on here at all. Just another tortured soul trying to make a living."

Issy returned to the table and tossed the shots on the reject pile.

It was close to five by the time she had finished going through all the submissions. The has-some-potential pile was easily the biggest, and Issy wondered whether she had the energy to go through it again.

"You ready to call it a day yet?" she called to Helen.

"Yes please! There's a Weight Watchers ready meal with our names on it."

Issy wrinkled her nose. She supposed that the empty calories she consumed with all the wine she was drinking needed to be tempered by something. Although the thought of chips seemed more appealing right now.

The door opened, and she glanced over. A tall, sandy-haired man entered and surveyed the room, taking in the building chaos and the relative calm of the gallery area. He walked over towards Issy's table.

"I didn't make the cut then?" He reached out and touched the lighthouse pictures that sat on top of the pile next to the Post It note with *NO* in red capital letters.

Issy stared up at him and tried not to melt into his chocolate brown eyes. It seemed that Ben Hudson was rather attractive.

"Sorry, Ben, no you didn't." She turned away, trying not to think about how handsome he was. She shouldn't even be thinking about other men right now. There was no way she would change her mind about the pictures. They held too many memories. A sob caught in her throat. She pushed back her chair, and it clattered to the floor as she rushed out of the cafe and down towards the safety of the shore. She stood there, watching the sun set, trying to forget how much it reminded her of Joel's proposal. At least there wasn't a lighthouse to taunt her as well.

"Helen thought you might need this."

Ben's voice came from behind her, and she turned to see him holding a large paper cup of hot chocolate with whipped cream on top. Issy gave him a weak smile.

"She's right." She accepted the cup from him and sank down on to the sand. "I'm sorry, it's not that your pictures are bad," she began. "They just bring back a lot of memories for me."

Ben gave her a crooked smile. "You too?"

Issy frowned. What did he mean by that? Did he have a proposal story as well? She watched as Ben sat down next to her and trailed his hand in the sand.

"I don't normally tell my life story to someone I've just met," he said. "Particularly as they've just dissed my life's work."

Issy gave him a sideways glance. She hadn't expected him to share anything with her. She didn't even know him, apart from the fact that they seemed to share a similar experience of a certain lighthouse. One corner of his mouth turned up, and she knew he wasn't serious about his second comment.

"She was called Ruth." Ben paused and took a breath. "We were university sweethearts, moved in together and had just started work when Ruth got sick. She was diagnosed with Hodgkin lymphoma just before her twenty-third birthday. We made a list of everything she wanted to do, just in case things didn't work out, even though everyone told her it would be fine. Ruth wanted to go to the Channel Islands to see the lighthouse because her parents had taken her there as a kid and she loved it." Ben's voice cracked as he went on. "She never made it. There were some complications, and she passed away just a few weeks before we were due to go. I went on my own, for her sake, and took those pictures for her. I just wish she had got to see them." He couldn't look at Issy as he finished.

Issy immediately felt guilty for discarding the photographs. She reached over and touched the hand that was making patterns. "I'm sorry. That kind of puts my reasons into perspective." She briefly told him about what had happened with Joel. "It doesn't really compare, does it?"

Ben looked directly at her, his eyes glassy with unshed tears. "Same place, different memory, same outcome. We're both unhappy. Although I'm obviously more unhappy because you've rejected my pictures."

Issy returned his gaze, noting the glint in his eye. "I guess I could always reconsider and move them to a maybe."

Lighthouse Boy

Janet M Baird

There's a photo of us on the beach. Black and white. My mother must have taken it because the rest of us are there. My sister and I, two skimpy look-a-likes in striped swimsuits. We're digging with our small spades, bought from the cliff top shop. Serious-faced. My twin, Meg, just slightly less serious than me and five minutes older.

"Jen, if we were princesses, I'd be queen," she'd say. I couldn't ever change that.

My father is fully-clothed in a tweed jacket and flannels, his long angular legs humped in a beach-hire deckchair. He's reading a paper through his thick tortoiseshell glasses. A wind break separates us from the next family. I can remember the piercing east wind and the sand blowing against my bare legs. A typical moment in our fifties east coast holidays. A gaunt cottage chosen from the Dalesman in February, checked out in April, and finally visited in August. It was rough and basic, but to us it was summer holiday nirvana. I can remember the pipe smoke. It curled round the edges of our lives like a permitted fragrance.

It wasn't forbidden then. Of course later he paid the price. They said it was the smoking but we believed it was the desert dust. Second World War desert dust, the colour of my father's ex-army khaki shorts.

I think the sun must have shone that day on the beach.

But some days the sea fret rolled in off the North Sea and infiltrated the beach with her damp tendrils. The sand was deserted, and we took refuge in the amusement arcade or went on long, cold, wet walks. That was when we heard the foghorn. It was attached to the lighthouse, and when the mist came in, it boomed dolefully.

Above the beach, halfway up the rickety cliff steps, there was a beach cafe. It perched on the cliff, nudged into a niche in the grey mud. It was our job to go for tea. This meant queuing up at the high counter and asking for thick white mugs of tea. We pushed the money over the counter and carried the tin tray back down to the beach. The mugs slid and grated across the sandy tray. By the time we had made it down the steps and across the sand to our camp, the tea was cold and tasted ever so slightly salty.

I saw the boy our age just as we were making the tricky transition from the steps to the sand. He was searching around the boulders at the cliff base. Probably fossiling, like most of the other small boys on the beach. The east coast was rich in ammonites buried in the shallow shackle and rocks. Thin and wearing frayed black jeans cut off below the knee, he had a grey t-shirt on which flapped in the stiff breeze. We didn't say hello or hi. He just looked at us, and we looked at him. He didn't meet our eyes but stared at us curiously. Twins always got stared at, and we were used to it. He went back to his fossiling. His movements were automatic and almost frantic as he clawed at the damp red cliff clay.

"Careful," I said as the tray swayed dangerously in Meg's hands. She'd carried it down the steps so it was my turn to transport the tea across the beach. We always took turns. It was an unspoken thing. The tray changed hands, and we set off slowly towards our windbreak. It was bright orange and striped so it was easy to spot from the sea of other windbreaks. I could sense the boy's eyes following us.

"Is he watching us?" I asked.

My twin checked quickly with a backwards dart of her head.

"Yep."

I didn't react but concentrated on reaching our destination. We weren't interested in boys. Or girls. As a compact unit of two, we didn't need friends. Especially not boys.

I didn't see the boy again until two days later. The weather deteriorated and the dreaded haze descended. The beach was out of the question. I kicked moodily at the tyre of our old green Austin car. It had a nose like a metal bulldog and shabby leather seats which stuck to your bare legs when it was hot. Not that it was hot now. The fog clung to the trees around the cottage and smudged the outline of the five-bar gate which sealed us off from the farm next door. There were three children there and a litter of Labrador pups. That was paradise to us. We actually just wanted to stay and play, but that wasn't an option. We always went out for the day, whatever the weather. Mum made packed lunches, from rolls and ham bought at the nearest small shop.

Today was a walk. The least favourite of our outings. Wet weather walks meant Wellies, waterproofs, and mud. The drive to the start of the walk was gloomy. We didn't even want to play car games. The cliff top car park was deserted and windswept. I got out reluctantly and changed into my black Wellingtons. All Wellingtons were black then, unless they were the green ones posh people wore. Ours had dishcloth-coloured insides which soaked up water if it dropped down from your legs. Our wellie socks were pull-on grey slippers which looked like dead mice.

Once we were booted up, we cinched in our gaberdines around the waist. I looked at my twin, and we set off resolutely. At that point, we didn't know we were walking to the lighthouse. As the path climbed out of the car park it narrowed to a track with wooden steps carved into the cliff side. Once we got to the top, the path widened out and we could see the lighthouse. It was dangerously near the cliff edge. The sea jumped and leapt at the lighthouse like a glittering tongue. White railings sealed the lighthouse off from the path. It was low and squat, not like the usual tower lighthouse you saw in the Ladybird reading books.

"L for Lighthouse," said Meg, reading my mind as usual. A twin thing.

"But it's not tall," I said, staring at the white and black dumpy tower. There was a house stuck on the end. No upstairs.

The top railing was around the height of our nine-year-old chins. We stared over curiously as we waited for our parents to catch up. A boy was playing by the door of the house. He ran back and forth with his head back and his elbows working like steam engine pistons. I looked more carefully as the boy stopped for breath.

"It's him."

We both stared. It was him. The boy from the beach cafe. The one looking for fossils in the cliff side.

"He's a lighthouse boy."

We watched the boy as he ran down to the end railings and tagged them before running back the other way, like a swimmer doing lengths of a municipal pool. Again his movements were automatic, almost compulsive.

Our parents caught up, and we ran off ahead, completely in unison.

The path stretched on towards the woods as it curved inland. Rooks clawed and swooped above as the trees moved in and shrouded the daylight out. We shivered, at some intangible terror, and waited half-paralysed until our parents caught up. We simultaneously slipped our hands into our parents' hands. My father's fawn gaberdine smelt damp but reassuring.

We didn't mention the lighthouse boy until that night. The cheap chintz curtains failed to keep out the summer light in our bedroom.

Our narrow twin beds were squashed into a small bedroom meant for one. The cottage was supposed to sleep six but four was a squeeze.

"So he lives with his parents."

"And he saves ships."

"And makes the light go on."

"And off."

There was a sleepy silence.

"And he sees whales..."

The late evening light faded, and we drifted off into questioning sleep.

We didn't go to the lighthouse again until the end of our holiday. We almost wanted it to rain. The days stretched on, unnamed. We were running out of time. Until at last we had a chance to visit the lighthouse boy again.

You could tell by the morning light in our bedroom there was a sea fret. We knelt on the window bed and peered out from behind the curtains. The shed in the yard was fronded with mist, and the sky was dull grey.

"Lighthouse," we said.

We hung round the car in our Wellingtons as Mum and Dad stowed the car with thermos flasks and sandwiches. Picnic lunches were always eaten outside the car, however cold it was. We climbed into the back and waited to leave. Mum put her head in the back door and looked curious.

"You're keen. Usually you don't like walks."

Secret looks.

Once we reached the car park, we were first out of the car. Our Wellingtons sploshed in the mud as we galloped off.

"Twins! Wait!"

But we didn't. Even though the word 'twins' was a warning.

"He's called Phillip," said Meg as we pounded along. We gave names to everyone we met.

I wouldn't accept that.

"No. He's in *The Mountain of Adventure*. He can't be in the lighthouse too."

There wasn't an argument. We lived in the fiction world of Enid Blyton and at the moment we were heavily into her adventure series.

We'd reached the bend just before the lighthouse. As one, we skidded to a halt. I closed my eyes. He had to be there. We walked around the bend with our fists furled up into tight balls. The mist swirled and drifted around the light-house, making it difficult to see. But the boy was there. He ran up and down by the fence with his head back.

"Why does he run like that?" puzzled my twin.

There was no answer. Unless we asked him.

We walked up to the gate, placing our boots down carefully as if tracking a wild animal in a jungle.

We always took turns to be more daring and outgoing, and on this holiday I was the more dominant twin.

I stepped up to the front gate as the boy approached it. "Hello?"

He swerved and looked at us but then ran on. He stopped just before the end fence and turned to run past us.

"Why are you running?" Meg asked.

The boy stopped again and stared at us. He came over to the black iron gate in the centre of the railings.

"I always do."

I stepped forward, mentally pushed by Meg.

"I'm Jen. This is my sister, Meg."

Meg moved forward, making sure she was just behind me. So much for being queen.

"What's your name."

The boy stared at us in turn.

He opened his mouth but no words came.

The three of us were locked in a static moment of observation and calculation.

I heard my voice break the silence.

"Have you seen the whales?"

Another long silence as we weighed each other up.

The whales were a huge part of our east coast holidays. From an early age we had stared up at the jawbone of a whale caught by the famous Captain Cook. It was hung up at the top of the cliff.

I could never accept it was a real whale.

Again the boy didn't seem to be looking at us, but his eyes rolled.

"I talk to them."

We stopped breathing.

A voice from the house made us all jump.

"Phillip! Get inside. Now!"

We reeled with shock. The boy *was* called Phillip. The boy twisted around and stared over to the lighthouse. His shoulders were anxious and angular, like the wooden coat hangers which hung on the wire in our cottage bedroom.

He skittered away like an anxious rabbit, without saying goodbye.

A woman pulled him inside roughly and slammed the door shut.

I looked at Meg. We didn't need to speak. The lighthouse boy needed help. He needed rescuing.

"Twins!"

Our parents approached. Our eyes met.

I decided to risk it. Jump the big divide, ask an adult to come into our world. Sort it. Make it better.

"Daddy," I said quickly. "That boy. He..."

Meg came to my rescue.

"He just runs up and down."

"And he sees whales. Daddy, he does."

Our father looked puzzled. He struggled at times to understand what his nine year old daughters were saying or thinking. Parents were far more distant then.

"I shouldn't worry. Children do that sometimes."

We trailed after our parents, feeling disappointed. It had been a huge leap of faith to confide in our parents and the result wasn't satisfying. But that's how it was then. Our parents didn't discuss issues like mental health with us. There was a girl at our primary school who screamed and had to be restrained. We were frightened but one day she wasn't there any more and the other children said she'd been locked away. She was never mentioned again.

The walk went on as if nothing had happened. We made it back to the car, ate egg sandwiches outside in the cold afternoon mist, and drove back to the cottage. Without sunshine it wasn't a happy place. We shivered in our bedroom as we pulled on our jumpers. Our Enid Blyton books lay by our beds. I was reading *The Castle of Adventure*. My twin was halfway through *The Valley of Adventure*.

"It was Philip," insisted my twin.

"But where was Lucy? And the others?"

My twin's face crumpled as she confused reality and imagination.

"We could be them?" she said.

The whole scenario hovered uncertainly for a few seconds.

I shook my head.

"No. But we could rescue him?"

The world stopped again but for different reasons.

There was no time to start the rescue plan, as tea was ready.

That night our bedroom was cold and draughty. A piercing wind fingered its way through the cracked window panes and thin curtains.

We were both lying on our fronts, with our despondent heads propped on our hands.

"We have to get him out of there."

"Get him back here. In the boot."

"Save up food."

Just how we were going to get the lighthouse boy back to our house in Yorkshire wasn't a worry. Yet.

My twin tipped over the side of her low cottage bed and peered underneath.

"He can live under my bed."

I inspected under my bed.

"Or mine."

We both rolled over to our backs and stared at the ceiling. It was light grey with spidery cracks running across it and a thick ugly light fixture dangled down in the centre.

Footsteps came up to our door. We stiffened and slumped into our we-are-fast-asleep mode. The trouble with this cottage was it had no stairs. It was a straggly line of add-on rooms.

No-one came in so we relaxed and rolled sideways and stared at each other.

"It has to rain tomorrow. It has to."

Sleep invaded. We couldn't resist it any longer.

Of course the next day was wall to wall bright sunshine. We went reluctantly to the beach. Our only hope was that the lighthouse boy might be at the beach cafe. We trailed up the wooden steps in the hot sun and collected our tin tray from the cafe.

I checked the cliffs either side of the cafe.

"He's not here," I said.

Meg narrowed her eyes and scanned the cliff side.

"No."

We knew we'd failed in our mission. I'd spotted the suitcases out in the hall before we left for the beach, and there was a suspicious cardboard box on the kitchen floor. We'd lost track of the days, but it must be almost time to go home.

The cafe owner cleared her throat.

"Yes? I haven't got all day."

I pushed the tin tray over the counter.

"Four teas."

My twin plonked the money on the counter.

"We could leave a note?"

The cafe woman looked confused.

"Sorry? You've given me the money?"

We looked down and avoided her. Neither of us spoke.

She pushed the teas over and put the change on the tray.

"You two off tomorrow?"

I stared at her in disbelief.

"What day is it?"

She laughed.

"It's Friday. Everyone goes home on Saturdays."

We took the tea back to our beach camp. Our sadness was tangible.

The cafe woman had confirmed our worst wishes. The cottage holiday was over and we had no chance of going back to the lighthouse.

Tea that night was all the leftovers. We called it eat ups. It was a family tradition, but we couldn't enjoy it. Packing was in full flow, and we knew it would be an early start in the morning. We were bundled off to bed while the grown-ups packed the food away and started loading the car. The cottage would be cleaned to within an inch of its life before we left.

We slumped on to our beds. The sheets would come off in the morning and go back in the car tied up in a turban like bundle. It was all very final.

Meg turned over.

"He's just going to die in there, Jen."

"He won't die. She'll just keep him locked up."

We knew it was hopeless. We had no transport and no power.

"We could write. Just put the Lighthouse Boy on it."

We lay in silence until sleep took over.

The next morning was frantic. As the car left the cottage and turned on to the lane, we knelt on the worn leather seat and stared out at the sea receding in the back window. It was another family ritual.

"Bye bye, sea," I said. My twin said nothing. But I knew what she was thinking.

We didn't write. I got as far as looking for our old toy post office set but all the envelopes were scribbled on. There was no way we could ask our parents for writing paper without saying why. The weeks stretched on and slowly the lighthouse and the boy faded in our memories. We didn't go back to the cottage the next summer. We didn't go on holiday at all. Our father's health worsened, and he was in and out of hospital. That summer we just played in our back garden.

I bounced our tennis ball off the brick wall of our semi and thought about the beach. And the lighthouse boy.

"D'you think he's still there?"

My sister shrugged. We were wearing identical navy blue shorts and patterned jumpers because even in July, Yorkshire is cold.

"He has to be. There's no way he could escape."

My sister caught the tennis ball and bonged it dismally against the back wall.

"We could run away?"

Before I could answer, the back door flew open and our mother appeared, looking dishevelled in her flowery apron.

"Twins, don't do that, please. Daddy's tired."

We froze in horror. At ten we had no idea that our actions might upset anyone. I pushed the tennis ball into my shorts pocket, and we retreated to our den down the garden. Suddenly our summer didn't seem exciting any more.

We didn't go back to the east coast for two years. We lost our father that summer and we were packed off to Scotland to an aunt, but we were disastrously homesick. The next year we did go to the coast, but none of us were interested in walking to lighthouses. We stayed in a thirties bungalow in Whitby. It wasn't the same. Adolescence clouded our brains, and the lighthouse boy was forgotten. We mooched in the amusement arcades and trudged up the steps to the west cliff to the Captain Cook memorial. We stared up at the jawbone of the whale.

I felt some deep down memories stir. When you are twelve, two years is a long time.

My twin walked around the memorial. My mother stared out to sea wistfully. I joined her at the flaked painted railings.

She shook her scarfed head.

"Are there still whales here," I asked.

Mum frowned out to sea.

"Of course not. Not now."

I pushed the memory of the lighthouse boy even deeper down.

Meg came back around to our side.
"Can we have ice creams, Mum?"

~~~

Fast forward many years.

I'm on my own. I'd need a book to tell the whole story, but my twin is no longer physically with me. We both developed eating disorders in our late teens eating and it took its toll. I lost my twin when we were in our early fifties. I'm trying to move from the unsatisfactory flat where we ended up after our mum's house was sold. My best friend tells me about an exciting house on one of those property programmes.

"I think it's where you used to go on holiday?"

I didn't recognise the lighthouse at first. The house bit was just a row of rooms, dressed up for TV. But it was the lighthouse. Undeniably. The windblown presenter stood outside the door and told us it was now a holiday cottage now up for sale. Way out of my single fifties price range. The presenter was pointing out to sea.

"They say you can see whales from here."

The sea glittered in a thin blue line on the horizon and just for a single second a boy ran across the screen. I stared and rewound the clip with shaking fingers. It couldn't be him. It didn't add up. I switched off and slumped back on our cheap faux leather settee.

I could hear the shouts as my twin and I ran down the cliff track, our black Wellies squelching in the mud. I could see the boy as he ran up and down the confines of the lighthouse garden. I could feel the bitter wind biting into our legs as we braved it out on the beach. I could hear the gritty slide of the tea mugs on the cafe beach tray. That's what memory does, doesn't it? It replays your life on constant repeat. Only mine is in stereo. The black and white photograph was on my coffee table. I'd dug it out of a carrier bag after I'd watched the programme. It was exactly the same. We were the same. Only now I was the only one here.

And what of the boy, the lighthouse boy. Where was he? Alive? Dead? Or cooped up in some kind of institution. Where he couldn't run. Or hear the sea. Or talk to whales. Miles away from the lighthouse.

A Slip in Time

Yvonne Parsloe

Mya slammed the door closed, setting off into the wood, dry autumn leaves crunching beneath her boots. Tugging her coat tighter against the breeze and shoving her hands deeper in the pockets, she trudged along.

In the ten years she had been absent from the family home, the woods hadn't changed a bit. Other than the echoes of happy family time.

Her brother now lived with his own little family on the other side of the world. Dad, Mum, and her sister Gilly had died in a car crash a couple of years before. Now she had come home to lick her wounds from a bad relationship.

The sound of heavy footsteps made her jump, glancing around she couldn't see anyone. The locals used the woods as a place to stroll, but she hoped not to see them.

Mya carried on to the glade in which she and her siblings had played, standing in the centre she closed her eyes and imagined their games of castles and swords. There was another little boy there for a while, but he had disappeared one day as suddenly as he had arrived.

The oak trees were old and gnarly. She wondered what stories they would tell if they could. A couple of the trees had fallen, baring their roots to the sky. The sound of footsteps and shouts touched her ears but no-one appeared.

Mya spotted the big tree under which a small cave hid, moving forward she peered into the dark. She wondered if it would feel smaller now that she was grown.

Stepping into the dark, she scuffed the ground with her boot. The dark closed round her, making her feel safe.

Drawing in a deep breath, she smelt smoke and heard the sounds of voices again. She gathered her courage to face whoever it was.

She propelled herself out of the cave from beneath the tree and stopped. A group of men sat around a fire. The trees were smaller, and the grass was deep and lush. The men wore tunics with swords and axes on their hips. She went to step back into the dark but was spotted by a man. She gasped. He was ruggedly beautiful with full lips, deep blue eyes, and broad shoulders. He grabbed up a sword and came towards her. Backing up, she felt her back bump into a body.

"Viggo shall we take this little woman with us?"

The man facing her came closer, he raised a hand to her hair and touched it.

"I wonder what tribe she belongs to. Yes, Thane, we will take her."

Mya's eyes widened at his words. Then the man behind shoved her forward. The man called Viggo enclosed her in his thick arms. Wriggling, she pushed the immovable man. He chuckled.

"How dare you manhandle me," she said. She kicked at his shins and still he just chuckled.

"My little captive you have spirit. What is your name? Come and sit."

He let her go, and she tried to dart away. The men, who were now all on their feet, bounced her from one to another until she was face to face with Viggo. Tears filled her eyes; tendrils of fear wound themselves about her.

Viggo saw the fear and shouted at the guffawing men to stop. They sat again and continued their chatter. He looked down at Mya. When she tried to return to the cave, he didn't stop her. With a sigh of relief, she was engulfed by the dark.

Heart pounding, she willed the sounds of them away. They didn't go for a while, and she waited in silence. When all was silent, she stepped back out to see the fire still smouldering. Glancing at the trees, she knew she was still away from home.

Plonking herself by the fire, she placed her hands over her face. The crashing of ocean waves reached her ears. It didn't make sense. The man called Viggo appeared, his hands held out no sword.

"What tribe are you from?" he asked.

"I live here. But something is wrong. The trees are too small, and I think I can hear the ocean."

"The sea is through the woods about one hundred feet. It is rough today, that's why you can hear it."

He sat opposite her.

"What movie are you in?" she asked.

"Movie. What is a movie?"

She shook her head. What the hell was going on? He stood and held out a hand.

"Come with me. Night will be drawing in. You can't stay here."

She shook her head, not wanting to go with the stranger. The wind blew hard, whipping her coat open. Struggling to pull it together, she felt a blanket come around her shoulders.

"Here, this will help you keep warm."

When she looked at him, she saw he was lacking

anything on his torso but a fine cotton shirt. She offered the tunic back. He shook his head, pushing it back towards her.

"Maybe you had better take me wherever you were heading," she said.

He strode ahead, and Mya followed until they broke through the trees. The sea raced across the shingle with a swoosh, touching his soft boots with its fingers of foamy water. She squealed when the water washed towards her. He swept her up and over his back.

From her upside down position she saw the shingle give way to shale and then grassy terrain. The sounds of people going about their lives came closer.

"What do you have there?" a loud male voice said.

A resounding slap hit her backside.

With little ceremony, Mya was dumped on her feet.

"Leave her alone," Viggo growled, socking the man.

Viggo grabbed Mya's hand and tugged her to his tent, dropping the flap into place.

"Sit."

He sat in front of her after she had taken the chair he had indicated.

She dropped her gaze to her fingers, picking at an invisible thread on her jeans. Placing a finger under her chin, he lifted her gaze.

"What is your name?"

"Mya."

Food was brought in by a surly looking woman.

"What are you going to do with her? Trade her?" the woman asked.

"Mind your own business woman."

The woman waited silently while Mya ate the food, then snatched up the dishes and stormed out with muttered curses. He glanced at Mya, caught her staring, and grinned before eating more of his own food.

The soft, fair stubble on his face caught the light. Mya reached out and touched it. He whipped his head around, making her jump. He chuckled. Taking her trembling hand, he lifted it to his face again.

"Your hands are soft."

He touched her jet black hair then held it, tugging her to him. He kissed her hard. She hauled back and slapped his face hard. He caught her hand and pulled her in again, the kiss softer this time.

When she was free of his grasp, she backed away and ran. Fear fuelling her legs, no-one touched her as she swerved through the village.

Viggo was hot on her heels. The sea she ran towards was rolling in high and fast.

"Wait," he called.

She ran harder, trying to get along the beach and into the bowl shape glade. Viggo was gaining on her. The tide was so high she started to run through it, lost her footing, and fell, soaked to the skin. Viggo pulled her to standing.

A shout of, "Traders," stopped both Mya and Viggo, who gazed out to the point of land on which a warning beacon appeared like an early lighthouse to steer ships safely into the cove from the glittering sea.

He dragged her back to the tent encampment.

The women and children, along with Mya, were sent into the largest tent. Clothes were brought to Mya by an older woman, and after changing Mya was guided to a mat. The seas were rough, and the traders wouldn't make landfall until morning.

The sun filtered through the shuttered canvas windows, thin lines fanned across the covers. Mya opened her eyes, staring straight into the sky-blue eyes of Viggo on a mat beside her. The night had passed without incident. The camp was now stirring for the day.

Men worked outside the encampment gathering wood for the fire until the traders began up the beach from their ship. Mya approached Viggo as he watched the trader's progress.

"What are you doing? Get back inside. If they see you they will try to take you from here. They steal what they can't trade for."Catching her arm, he pushed her back towards the village. She shrugged him away with an angry scowl.

"Now, little captive. That scowl doesn't suit you."

"What would you know suits me?"

He chuckled and tilted her chin, gazing down at her, a quirk of a smile on his lips. He placed a finger to her mouth for her to be quiet.

"I know you better than you think." He walked out to greet the traders, men with red hair and beards.

Mya watched through the gap in the flap of Viggo's tent, intrigued, wondering if they were Vikings too. Two of the traders had slipped away from the centre and disappeared from view.

Mya sighed and retreated back into the warmth, plonking herself on the mat to wait for the traders to go. The voices were still mumbling away, and she grew tired of waiting. Laying down, her lids became heavy and a deep doze fell over her.

A hand covered her mouth. She tried to scream.

"Don't scream or I'll slit your throat,"the red-haired man said. He placed a blade to her neck to prove the point, digging it slightly to dent her soft skin. Propelling her out of the tent in front of himself, the trader yelled, "Who is this little pretty?"

His leader glanced up and grinned. "I thought you said the only women here were these old ones," he said to Viggo.

"She is my woman," Viggo stated.

Anger marred the rugged face of Viggo when he saw the blade digging at Mya's skin. With a roar, he jumped to his feet. The trader pressed the knife harder and drew blood.

"I'll slit her throat if you come closer."

Viggo halted and snarled. "You will pay for drawing her blood, however little."

Viggo whistled loudly and his men surrounded the traders, leaving the trader with the knife isolated from his cohorts.

Mya didn't wait for help. She kicked the man hard in the shin with the heel of her boot. He yowled, but the knife slid across her neck. Viggo threw his small dagger. It hit the trader square in the shoulder, causing him to drop the knife. The trader leader tried to grasp Mya, who aimed a kick at his gut and made him bend, giving her room to run towards Viggo.

He caught her and swung her around, using himself to shield her.

"Leave now. If you value your lives. Leave the one who drew her blood. Go!" Viggo shouted.

The traders were escorted to the shore, except for the one who had hurt Mya.

Viggo sat Mya down and checked her wound. Anger creased his features while he cleaned and covered the thin line on her throat.

"Mya. I'm sorry you got hurt." He held a hand to her cheek.

She leaned into his hand and closed her eyes. For the first time in years she felt cared for.

A blood curdling yell came from the other end of the camp. Mya bolted upright.

"What is it Mya?"Viggo asked.

He held out a hand, palm up, a gesture of friendliness. Tucking her legs up she hugged her knees, keeping as much distance as possible between them.

"You hurt that man?"

"No, not hurt. He paid for damaging you. It was an insult."

He moved his hand closer; she shook her head, and he dropped it.

"It is our way. You are mine. Other tribes will hear of you and how I dealt with it and it will keep you safe."

Mya thought about this for a moment. Viggo slumped onto a stool next to her. Placing her hand on his where it rested on his thigh.

"Thank you for protecting me. If you showed me how to get back, then you would have no need of worrying about me."

"The slip has closed. It could be some time before it reopens."

Mya was shocked to hear he knew how she had appeared.

"I have a tale to tell you Mya. You are part of it. When I was a boy I went through the slip. I got stuck for a few years. A family took me in."

He paused; she stared at him.

"My family took you in. I remember. Mum said you should stay until we found out where you had come from," she said.

"When you popped out of the cave, I saw those big

brown eyes full of fear. A look I had seen before when we went up to the lighthouse. You were terrified of heights."

Her eyes filled with tears. "A couple of days after that you disappeared."

He wrapped her in his big thick arms. She snuggled against him.

"Are your family well?"

She sniffled, memories of her losses hit her. He tightened his hug.

"My parents and sister died in a car crash three years ago. My brother has his own family and lives on the other side of the world."

For a long while they sat like this.

"Stay here with me. Our boats will come, and we will go to my homeland," he said.

Mya smiled at him. When he bent his head to kiss her, she felt like she was home.

Hidden

Jennifer Syme

The woods are my home, mine and Mother's. I know every inch of them, or at least the part I am allowed to go to. I can go as far as the big fallen tree to the east, the river to the west, the tree with the mark on it to the south, and the cliff to the north. Other directions have got markings on trees as well, but they are so dense with bushes and spiky branches no-one can get through them anyway, not even me. Mother made them to tell me my limits. When I was younger, I never ventured even that far, but now I am older I go right to the edge as often as I can. I peer past the invisible barrier and wonder what is out there, what it is that I must not see.

Or, as Mother says, what mustn't see me.

For I am different.

Trouble is, I don't know why.

I can see I am different from Mother, and she has told me that everyone else is like her, and that people like me have been taken away and put in special places. Or worse. When I ask her, she has two responses. The first is that she looks scared and whispers to me that I must just believe her, that we will have problems in the future but that she has a plan. Meanwhile I *must not* go past the boundaries. I prefer that version of her reaction. The other times she has looked at me in a way that makes my insides go weird, like I might need to go outside and use the toilet. She looks like the bear we met once that had cubs. Its eyes went black, and it stood there, massive, growling a deep, furious growl and ready to kill. *That* is how mother looks.

So I don't question her anymore.

Apart from the boundaries, I am pretty happy with our life in the woods. We have vegetables, chickens, our horse Red for mother to ride, and Bob the dog to keep me company when Mother goes off hunting or on her trips to where other people are. I am learning to hunt as well as being in charge of the vegetable patch now.

I go out every day to hunt or just to explore, discover new plants and see what birds and animals are about. I have my favourites that I check on, my special places where I can hide for hours, watching them and learning their habits. I have a set path, and Bob and I check each place in order every week, sometimes more than once.

Of course there are other rules I have to stick to as well.

No noise, we must not be heard.

Oh, and if I see a person, I must hide or run away. On no account must I go up to them, speak to them, wave, or even smile.

I have seen people, once. The first time I followed Mother into the woods. The time before she caught me and turned into a mother bear. The first time, I hid in bushes and watched her talking to a group of people and exchanging vegetables for meat and laughing with them. It made me feel strange to see her with others.

Yesterday she called me over from where I was filling the basket with kindling at the wood store. "Kris. I have to go to the town tomorrow, get some things. I'll be away a night. Ok?"

I nodded, trying to look suitably blank-faced. It was

normal, she did this every now and then, we could only supply ourselves with so much, so she went to trade or sell things, sometimes with other people who lived near the woods and sometimes she went farther to the town, when she had to stay overnight. She didn't do that as much; she didn't like leaving me alone.

This time though, I had plans. I thought if I climbed a particular tree, I would see what was on the other side of the river. I was sure I'd smelled smoke the last time I was there. I wanted to see if there was another house over the other side.

She turned away. "Usual rules apply, Kris. You do your jobs and you stay at the house, yes?"

She glanced back at me, and I nodded again. "Yeah, I know. Me and Bob will be fine."

Today I waved her off, Red's large backside disappearing through the thick trees, the path barely wide enough for him. As soon as they were out of sight, I clicked my fingers at Bob to follow me and set off in almost the opposite direction.

I made fast progress to the tree, getting to my boundary before my stomach told me it was lunchtime. I scrambled up using a smaller tree to access the lower branches of the large one, and once I was in its dense crown, it was quite easy for me to scramble almost to the very top. Mother always called me a little monkey child because of my tree climbing. She had shown me pictures of monkeys in far off places.

Once I was at the top, I peered out over the river. Farther down it was quieter, and we fished in it sometimes, but here it was fast, coming down from the waterfall up in the cliffs.

I looked where I thought I had seen smoke before and at

first couldn't see anything, but then there it was. A faint whisper of white smoke—a fire. People. I wasn't sure how far away it was; I knew it was farther than it looked, but it gave me a chill of excitement, and also fear, was this why mother told me to keep quiet? People were not that far away? I had always thought we were so well-hidden, that no-one else was anywhere nearby.

I slithered back down the tree and clicked my fingers again for Bob, but instead of setting back on the direct route, or even on my usual path, which followed the animal tracks, I headed down river. My head buzzed with the idea that I had just seen proof of other people. I was determined to see if I could spot anything else. I was still on our side of the river, and it was too wild here to cross, so I wasn't disobeying Mother.

I got to a spot where I could see the other side, but there was still plenty of dense coverage for me to be concealed. I stared over to the other bank, up and down as far as I could make out in each direction. It was peaceful there, with the sun warming my head from above and the sounds of the river tumbling by and the birds and insects going about their business. I must've fallen asleep because the next thing I knew, Bob was growling in my ear.

I opened my eyes and looked at him. He wasn't growling at me but was staring over the river, his nose poking into the bush in front of us. I peeked through too, and there was a person, like mother, with another dog on the other side. I shrank back into the bush and patted Bob.

"Shhh Bob," I said in a whisper. He sat back; Mother had us both well trained.

I watched, fascinated, as the woman walked down the river, occasionally talking to the dog. She didn't seem to be doing anything in particular. She was dressed in the same way we did, her hair tied back with a large hat on her head. She carried a small bag on her back, much like mine. Eventually she started to head back into the woods, and just then she turned, and for one second I felt like she was looking right at me, somehow seeing through the bushes. I shrank back, my stomach heaving, and fear buzzing through me. I had an urge to run, but I made myself sit until I was sure that she had gone back into the woods on her side, my breath coming in shallow gasps. Then, I forced myself to crawl slowly back and away from the river.

I wanted to get back to the house, so we headed back and I did my chores and cooked myself some eggs and vegetables, making sure everything was tidied up afterwards. My head was busy thinking: There were people not that far away, I had always felt safe but now I didn't know what to feel. Mother had made it very clear that other people meant danger for me, but I didn't understand why. She just said I was 'special', but I don't feel special. I know I am different from Mother. I can see that, but I don't see what is wrong with me. I can speak, I can see, hear, run; I have all my arms and legs.

I asked once if she would like to be nearer other people, if we didn't have to be hidden, and she had paused a long time and then said, "No Kris. I like being here, doing my own thing. I don't think I'd have liked how it used to be when everyone lived in towns and there were too many people. It was all before my time too, Kris, you know that, but from what I know, the Change and the new order was a good thing. Less people, more space and things getting back into balance." Then she had looked at me and added, "But there are things that I don't like, and I hope those things might change before too long."

Mother had said she would be one night, so when she hadn't returned by dinner time the following night, I felt a bubble of fear form in my throat. I went as far along the path as I was allowed and climbed up a tree to watch out for her. Then I went back and ate the food I had prepared and spent another night alone, although I didn't sleep much.

After two more sleepless nights, the bubble was now threatening to choke me. I spent the entire day up the tree staring along the path.

She had never been gone this long. Never.

She had told me that if she didn't come back I must stay hidden, carry on doing what we did. Survive. I had dismissed it; of course she would come back, why wouldn't she? I refused to consider the options, and the outcome, if she didn't.

The third day, I decided I had to go and look for her. She might've fallen on the path; Red could've got a fright and thrown her. With shaking hands, I packed a small bag with food and also some things from Mother's medicine cabinet. She had tablets and bandages in there, also some needles and syringes. I had no idea what they were for. "Emergencies" was all she had said when I asked.

I set off, Bob at my heels. My excitement of the other day when I went exploring replaced by a knotted stomach and trembling legs. I got to the boundary tree and hesitated. Beyond the bend at the tree the path got wider; our path looked like a deer track into the bushes from the other side. This was the way to people. I decided to go on the path but to be ready to hide at first sight or sound of anything. It would be quicker than trying to scramble alongside it in the bushes.

We made good progress and saw or heard nothing to

make me hide. I stopped for some water and an apple from my bag, and it dawned on me that I was now farther than I had ever been from the house. From safety. I could feel panic in my throat; it rose within me, threatening to erupt in a scream, a shriek into the woods.

Mother.

But she had taught me well. No noise. Be silent. Draw no attention. I had never shouted. Never yelled or screamed. I learned to be quiet almost as soon as I could make a noise. She taught me to hide, to conceal myself in bushes and behind trees. She taught me so much, but not to be alone, not to venture out like this.

When it got dark, I crawled into a dip hidden by bushes, and Bob nestled in beside me. I stared up at the sky, just like at home the trees were dense here, only patches of sky peeked through.

On the third night of sleeping under bushes, I realised that I could see more stars, more sky. The woods were changing, less dense, more low bushes. Different types of trees. The soil was changing too. It was lighter, grainier, here.

On the fourth day, I sat beside a small river. There were several of these throughout the woods, and I had been able to fill my water bottle. Tears dropped down my face. I had no idea where I was or what was ahead, but there was no sign of Mother, or Red. I knew I must be near the edge of the forest, that another day or two of walking would bring me to whatever lay beyond it. And whoever was there too. I didn't want to go any farther. Fear held me back; worry about Mother drove me forward. Again the desire to yell her name came over me, but I muffled my cries into my bag, and then Bob who came over to snuffle at me.

As I looked at the small stream, I thought about the

woman at the river, there were others like her, like us, out there. If only I could speak to them, get help.

Soon, I realised that the path was now running alongside a larger river. I thought about the directions and wondered if it was our river. It was flatter and moved differently here; there were no rocks and rapids for it to roar over. I stayed back in the trees, wary of what might be near it now.

Now I heard a sound—a whoosh and then a distant thump. I stopped. It repeated every few minutes. I carried on, picking my way carefully over the roots, keeping behind bushes. The earth was a lighter colour than I had seen before. The trees were farther apart. Above me I saw larger patches of sky, blue against the green of the leaves.

I stopped; I had come to the end of the woods. They ended and in their place were small hills—lumps, really— taller than me but not much. They weren't made of earth but a soft-looking, yellow substance that reminded me of something. The mounds were topped with long, thin, grass-like plants that grew in clumps. I crawled in between them and shuffled up towards the top where I peered through the grass. Bob whined but came with me.

"Ah." I made an involuntary sound; I'd never known grass this sharp. I had cut my finger slightly. I sucked it and peeked round the grass clump. In front of the mounds, there was an expanse of yellow, which spread away into the distance either side of me before disappearing out of sight. The ground rippled in the wind, and here and there little puffs and swirls appeared. At the same time there was a smell; a fresh, tingly sensation, and I had the urge to run across the yellow ground. My stomach knotted and fluttered. I knew what this was, Mother had this stuff on her boots when she went fishing at the lake that was too far for me to go to. I tentatively reached out and picked up a handful of the grains and rubbed some between my fingers. It was gritty but not sore, it tickled my palms. It was rougher than the dust on Mother's boots, but it was the same stuff. She had told me what it was. 'Sand', I whispered, 'Sand at the edge of the lake.'

I lay there and looked at the area in front of me, as the light danced across, it sparkled in the sun. I glanced up and realised that I saw sky, properly saw it. A blue expanse above my head, with swirls of cloud. I had never seen it like this. I stared up, my heart pounding. This was all so much to take in. What was this place? Was I at the lake? It didn't look the way Mother had described it.

The whoomph sound was different now I heard it out of the woods. It was less muffled; it had a splashy sound to it like the waterfall in the woods after heavy rain. I strained my neck upwards to see more, poking my head over the grass as much as I could without actually rising too far. In the distance was a different blue from the sky. This was moving with white areas rising and falling on top of it, and I realized they were waves. I'd seen pictures in mother's books, but they had been much smaller than these, which looked like walls of blue glass crashing down, making the noise I was hearing. The only thing I'd seen that was like it was the biggest waterfall on the river, which roared and crashed over the rocks. That was a chaos of movement, what I was seeing here was rhythmic, almost soothing in it's regularity.

"The sea," I whispered and was filled with a memory of a story Mother read me years ago about creatures that lived in the sea. She had said it was far, far away and we would never see it. But it was right there, in front of me.

In the story there had been fish in the sea, and people

had waded in it, playing and splashing in it. Swimming like we did in the lake pool.

I looked in either direction, raising myself up into a squat to see if it there was an end to the sea or the sand. In the distance there was a large rock with a white tower like the ones I had seen in other stories. I stared at it as it glittered like Mother's glass bird-scarers in the sun—a lighthouse. There had been one of those in the sea story too. Dimmed in the daytime, at night it would light up the sea for boats.

But Mother had said there were no boats now.

A slight wind puffed at me, and I caught the scent that had been at the edge of my senses, that tingly fresh scent. It gave me the urge to run towards the sea and put my feet in it, to splash and play like they had in the books.

Then I saw her, a woman on the beach, walking alone.

"Mother?"

The pull of the breeze, the sparkling sea, and the sight of her was too much.

It made me forget that I was meant to hide, that I was a secret. It made my legs act of their own accord and carry me over the warm yellow towards her.

Only when I got closer did I notice the hat on her head, and the dog that had been in her shadow.

About the Authors

Julie Archer

grew up in Hampshire and lived in Reading before moving to the beautiful riverside town of Dartmouth in Devon. She still feels like she's on holiday. Julie trained as a journalist, then went into teaching (kept meeting the sixth form students in the pub, awkward!). After that she 'fell' into recruitment, spending more years there than she cares to mention, where the most creative thing she did was to create a sexy top line for job adverts! Since moving to Devon, she set up her own business offering virtual administration and recruitment services, worked for an accommodation company and is currently moonlighting in the local bookshop...

Also, COYS, Cats, Metal. Underneath this preppy exterior beats the heart of a rock chick.

Julie released her first novel *Cocktails, Rock Tales & Betrayals* in 2016, which was followed by *One Last Shot*, the second story in the Blood Stone Riot rockstar romance series, in June 2017. She is currently working on a secret project in collaboration with a number of other romance authors. Go stalk her on Facebook if you want to find out more: facebook.com/juliearcherwrites/.

Janet M Baird

is a tutor and writer living in Yorkshire, England. She is writing a middle grade novel about mountain biking and also writes flash fiction, poetry, and short stories. Janet has been published in Mslexia. She has been interested in trains ever since she travelled up to Scotland on a steam train at the age of five. Recent train trips include New York Metro, Eurostar, and the Canadian Via train. Janet also travels regularly by train to London and uses the time for writing. She also finds an endless supply of new characters for her short stories!

Charlie Haynes

runs Urban Writers' Retreat, which gives people time and space to escape from the real world and just write. As well as running one-day and residential retreats, she creates online tools and structures to help writers, including The Writer's Playground, Writer's Block Detox, and The Six Month Novel with our editor Amie.

Basically, she helps writers to do their thing and feel good about it.

When she isn't looking after other writers, she writes gloriously craptastic speculative fiction. She's a digital nomad (or semidigital semi-nomad, perhaps) who sometimes lives off-grid, sometimes travels a lot, and is obsessed with baking and flying trapeze. Yes, the circus kind.

Sarah Jeffery

is a former journalist with many features and articles to her name. Now working in PR, she immerses herself in storytelling every day. Based in Newcastle upon Tyne, she is currently writing a collection of short stories. When she's not writing, she is most likely curled up on the sofa with a good book or at a concert as she is an avid gig-goer.

Amie McCracken

edits and typesets novels for self-published authors and helps new writers polish their work. She also runs the Six Month Novel with Charlie. She is an imaginist, with a lot of ideas floating around in her head and a long list of places still to visit. She's been swimming in books her whole life, therefore having a career as an editor and book designer was only natural. There's always a book or three on her nightstand and a manuscript in progress on her laptop. There's also a possibility she might be addicted to tea. Amie's books, *Emotionless* and *Blink*, are available at all major booksellers.

Yvonne Parsloe

was born in Hampshire and moved to Gloucestershire when she was very little. She has been a seamstress for more years than she cares to mention. And can boast thirty-three years of marriage with two grown children and four grandchildren. She has written ten novels to date but is still working on the edits. She has kept diaries for many years and dabbled with writing since she can remember.

If she's not writing then she is out with her hubby and dog, watching her son play football, or playing with her grandchildren. She lives a very ordinary life with a penchant for adventures lived through her stories.

Shanthi Sam

has been writing stories and poetry almost since she was able to write. She had tremendously supportive parents, so of course that turned her against the whole thing when she was a teen, and she didn't actually get back to writing until she was in her thirties. She's lucky enough to have a room with a view in Dubai, where she lives with her wonderful husband, and Berlioz and Makutsi, the cats. Her belief that truth is a liquid and takes the shape of its container is not connected to her belief that enough sangria can make anyone beautiful.

Jennifer Syme

lives in Fife, Scotland. She has always wanted to be a writer, but it is only in recent years she has actually started thinking of herself as one and putting words out into the world. Before that she studied environmental issues, worked as an Analyst/Programmer, and now works part-time as a sports massage therapist when she isn't writing. She writes and blogs about creativity and wellbeing and has a book on that subject available on Amazon. She has also had short stories published by Scottish Book Trust and is working on her first novel. When not working or writing, she plays guitar (electric, loudly), runs, mountain bikes and reads.

Jeannie Wycherley

stumbled across Urban Writers in June 2012, coincidentally at the same time she was made redundant. What further excuse did she need to drown herself in words? The Writers' Playground has afforded Jeannie the opportunity to develop both her creative skills and her procrastination techniques. In 2017, Jeannie has published her debut novel, *Crone*; an anthology of short stories, *Deadly Encounters*; and a non-fiction book about dealing with pet loss, *Losing my Best Friend*.

Jeannie lives in an area of outstanding natural beauty in East Devon in the UK and draws inspiration from the landscape—particularly the forests, the sea mists, and the rocky coastline. Given that she writes horror, make of that what you will.

The Writer's Playground

Writing isn't always easy, and there are some things we could all do with to help us along the way: accountability, motivation, support, and friendship. The Writer's Playground, from Urban Writers' Retreat, is an online home for writers that provides just that.

This anthology comes from a group of writers who spend their writing time in the playground, encouraging each other and generally procrastinating their work in a supportive way. But, as is obvious by this book in your hands, they also sit in the chair and get words on the page.

If you would like to find out more, or join in with other programmes run through Urban Writers' Retreat like residential retreats, the Six Month Novel, or other procratination-busting courses, visit the website at urbanwritersretreat.co.uk.

Acknowledgements

This book came about because a group of writers who sit day after day beavering away on their work, deserved to be published and belonged in a book together. They spend their time supporting each other, cheering each other on, and generally ruling the writing world. So here's a big thank you to the authors of these stories. For constantly checking in weekly, for being shoulders to cry on, for understanding each other.

A huge shout out needs to go to our proofreader. Paul Anthony Shortt, thank you so very much for contributing your expertise to this project. We hope you enjoyed correcting our grammar errors as much as we liked making them.

The proceeds of this book go to charity. Our chosen charity is the Ministry of Stories (ministryofstories.org) because fostering the next generation of writers is dear to our hearts. We feel that passing on our passion is incredibly important (and only a teensy bit selfish), and the way The Ministry of Stories brings imagination into daily life is beautiful. So thank you MoS for what you do and hopefully you can keep on keeping on for a long time.

If you liked these stories, please help other readers find them by posting a review on any of the major retailers.

If you would like to find out more about the editor, Amie McCracken, visit her website amiemccracken.com.